Thanks for all the support

— S. Collin Ellsworth

The House Joey Built

S. Collin Ellsworth

DEDICATION

To all who have experience pain and lost: May you find reason to continue
and a love that set you free.

CONTENTS

ACKNOWLEDGMENTS

I like to thank the Chanhassen Authors Collective and the Art Consortium of Carver County for all their work in supporting me and other Minnesota authors.

1

I read once you got to heaven, you'll be in your favorite place. Currently, I stand in Miles Creek during the three notable seasons of Minnesota. The rocks and waters crystal like ice, yet the water still flows. Purple flowers and yellow dandelions pop from the ground. Red and yellow leaves shower me without stripping the branches down to their wood skeletons. I feel no heat nor chill, only peace. I know I am in heaven.

"Pretty, isn't it?"

I turn to see a muscular man with longish black hair and a beard. He wears the black jacket and wrestling sweatshirt he wore during our failed escape. He was a lanky punk when he died. Now, he's the handsome man I knew he would have become.

"Joey!"

I run to him. The white vintage wedding dress I dreamt of wearing in my youth remains dry as my feet create splashes in the water. He smiles and opens his arms to me. I jump into his embrace giggling.

"Marion, it's good to see you."

"Oh my God, Joey! I can't believe it! You look so grown up!"

"I'm nearly forty! At least, I'm supposed to be. Like the beard?"

"It suits you."

For nearly twenty years, all I had of Joey were the ashes I received at his memorial. Now, I draw him close. His familiar scent of wood and fabric softener now mixes with marshmallows and fresh water. Heaven even smells like I dreamt it would.

Joey released me from our embrace and looks at me. Not to be deceived by his manly appearance, he reminds me of the eighteen-year-old who died by grabbing my breast.

"Finally, they came in!"

I laugh, grab his hairy chin and pull him into a kiss. Finally, the bliss I missed.

Suddenly, I feel a spark in my abdomen. With a great pull, I feel the baby I carried release from me. There it is, the perfect pink bundle I always wanted laying in the water next to me. I bend down and gather the child into the folds of my skirt. The baby smiles and gurgles joyfully as I raise it to Joey.

"Joey, meet Joey."

Joey laughs as he touches the baby's face. For seconds I enjoy the peace I sought in the creek my entire life.

Like all of my joys, it is short lived. Fire burns on my chest. I spasm. Joey grabs me again and takes Baby Joey with his other hand.

"I knew it wasn't your time," he whispers.

Electricity jolts my soul. Despite burying myself in Joey, I am pulled away from him. At the speed of light, I am sucked into the white light's vortex. With a hard landing, I am trapped again in my flesh, weighed down by excruciating pain. The sickening smell of disinfectant greets my nose. I reach for my stomach. I can feel a spiritual hole. I returned alone.

My tears sting my face. All I can muster is a small whimper, "Joey."

"You lost the baby, Marion."

Such a matter of fact voice my husband has. I learned a long time ago not to expect exclamations from Irving. Actually, I am surprised he is here. As if my soul can sink any further, I realize my father is here.

"A drunk driver hit you," Irving explained.

I closed my eyes. Could I go back to the creek?

I heard a woman's voice, "Mr. Palavar? The doctor needs to speak to you and Mr. Portwood."

Irving just leaves. He doesn't mention to whom I believe is the nurse that I woke up. That's fine. I wait until I no longer hear the clicking of their heels in the hallway. Deep from my soul, I scream from the pain.

2

Everyone needs a place to run to, a place to center themselves. I was lucky. Miles Creek was in my backyard. I jumped over my father's hedge border and entered the tree curtains leading to the park. I had many bad days with my father. I never lived up or understood the standards he had for me. I still don't.

Joey moved into his step father's apartment blocks away from me when he was eleven. Due to our neighborhood's proximity, we never would have met until high school if it weren't for the creek. I met him one day while walking too far from the house when I was ten. He was building a fort by leaning twigs against a tree. Before then, I never liked boys. That day, I stood transfixed on his olive skin and shiny black hair.

"You can come help me," he said when he noticed me.

I did. That "fort" was a solace for indulging our imaginations. Joey became the one friend that understood me. He made my world less lonely.

Later, it became a place for our misdeeds. Joey started bringing girlfriends to the fort. I brought cigarettes.

"I'd prefer you didn't smoke in the woods," he told me, "you're going to start a fire."

"I'd prefer you didn't bring sluts to woods," I'd retort. "It disturbs the peace."

We grew up, but never apart. Joey remained my friend even as he became the popular jock. We were to each other the one person we could be ourselves around. Still, being best friends didn't mean we never quarreled.

When I was seventeen, our banter came to a head. Another rough day with my father caused me to sneak out the backdoor. Daylight savings time started the weekend prior. I had an extra hour to smoke before it got dark. I jumped over the border ran through the skeletal trees. Mud clumped on my boots, and I cleaned them with the small remnants of snow. Using a fallen branch as a walking stick, I climb the hill.

Once I reached the top, I peeked into the fort. No Joey petting his latest ample bosoms. I entered pulled out my pack of menthols from the pocket of my fitted leather jacket.

"I told you not to do that here!"

Joey grabbed my pack from behind. With his hand around my wrist, he wrapped my arm around me. He slid his foot between my legs before I knew it I was sitting on the ground twisted into him.

"Jesus Christ, Joey! How long have you been here?"

"I've been waiting for you."

"Waiting? Why?"

"I saw you trying not to cry as you walked to the bathroom at school today. I put two and two together. I figured you must got cut from some academic team or fellowship and Daddy Portwood would rip you a new one. I can't have you burn down our sanctuary or worst, the entire area of the creek."

"I applied to take postsecondary courses at the College of Saint Catherine's next year. I didn't get accepted."

"So you will be stuck in high school your senior year?"

"Nicollet is an option," I replied, "However, I go to school to escape my dad. School won't be an escape if I attend the college where my father teaches. Now give me my cigarettes."

5

Joey let go of me and lifted my cigerettes above his head. I feebly jumped to retrieve them to no avail. Joey alternated between laughter and shaking his free finger at me. I sat in the front of the fort sticking my tongue out.

"If you refuse to give me back my cigarettes, I am not going to move. When your girl de jour arrives, you'll have no place to…."

Joey started to play catch with my pack. "There is no girl de jour."

I opened my mouth to say a pithy retort, but nothing came out. I watched Joey toss my cigarettes for five minutes until crushing them with his hands on the last catch. Then he threw them. He could throw a pitch despite being a wrestler rather than a baseball player. I leaped at him. Joey quickly spun around and jumped on top of me, pinning me down. Wet mud started oozing into my jeans.

"I'm not hurting you, am I?" Joey asked softly.

"No, but you're still making me angry. Get off of me!"

Joey complied. Towering over me, he shook his head. "I never understood how a smart girl like you resorts to smoking. You're not an idiot. You know they cause cancer. Of all the people I know, you are the least concerned about trying to look cool."

I scooted over to the entrance of the fort.

"I can say the same thing about you and STDs."

"I don't mess around as much as you think," Joey replied, "and when I do, I used condoms."

"You have your mode of escapism, and I have mine. Why do you care if I smoke?"

"Because smoking is for losers who skip class and hang at that the church parking lot next to the school. You're better than that."

I burrow my knees into my chest. "I am a loser. My ranking dipped into the three digit mark on my last report card."

Joey shakes his head. "It is all about Daddy Portwood. How 'low' his your ranking?"

"I am the 100th ranked student in my class."

Joey lifted his arms up in defiance. "100th out of a thousand students! What a travesty you rank in the top ten percent."

"At the bottom of the top ten percent," I pointed out. "I am not smart enough to obtain the opportunities my father wants me to pursue. I am not reaching high enough, yet I try so hard. I focus on school work until my nerves are fried. It feels like my spinal cord's been stripped after I do my homework. I feel my nerve endings fray."

"You're a good kid, Marion. Except for the smoking, you do nothing wrong. Why can't he let up on you!"

"That is why I smoke. The time I hide and have a cig is time where I can just shut down."

"There are other ways to calm down," Joey pointed out.

I laid down on the ground. Mud cushioned my neck and my beret covered head.

"You said it yourself; I'm a kid. I can't calm down like you do with your girlfriends. Guys only give their D to girls with big tits and long hair."

"So that is what you really wanted!"

I closed my eyes. Why did I just say that to Joey? I squeezed my eyes tighter hoping to will him to disappear. The sound of Joey's footsteps came closer to me. He bent down and put his hand on the center of my chest.

"Come on," he whispered.

I opened my eyes as Joey headed to the fort. He sat down inside and patted his lap. My body flushed a pink heat. I only got that feeling around Joey. I got up and walked to the fort. Joey reached for my hand when I reached him. Gently he lowered me onto his lap and cradled my torso with his left arm.

"May I?"

I nodded. He put his right hand underneath my jacket rubbing my small breasts. My body shuddered.

"They feel good enough for me," Joey said. "How about you?"

A soliloquy popped in my head. If it were any other guy, he'd be slapped across the face and burned with my lighter. Joey felt safe. His charting my body was natural. I couldn't say any of that. I could barely nod my head. With that, I felt him go underneath my ribbed turtleneck. I gasped as his hands frigid from the Minnesota air touched my bare belly.

"Too cold?"

I nodded.

"I know where girls love cold fingers touching them. May I?"

I nodded again before leaning my head back. Joey unzipped my jeans and slid his fingers underneath my panties. He slid his finger between the folds of my vulva. The friction of his touch warmed his icy finger as the heat radiated from me. Joey leaned his face close to mine.

"Feeling better?" he asked brushing is lips against mine.

I pressed my lips against him until a sensation vibrated throughout my body. Every molecule burst. My skin's response to touch became amped up to a point where I couldn't take it anymore. I leaped so fast to my feet; I left rub burn marks on Joey's wrist. He painfully chuckled. He motioned me to sit in his lap. He held me for a moment. A beeping sound disturbed our peace. Joey pulled out his beeper from his jacket pocket.

"It's my mom," Joey said. "She needs me to come home. Are you going to be okay getting home? It's getting dark."

"I don't live too far," I answered.

We got up. Joey bolted in the direction of his apartment. I headed home, but I took the longer trails. Everything buzzed around me. I felt giddy. I didn't want to go back to the reality of my existence. Finally, I was one of Joey's girls. I was special. I didn't need to go home and endure another lecture from my father to remind me I was average.

I stayed outside until my mother called out from the porch. Thankfully,

I was close enough to my yard. I emerged from the woods to my mom's silhouette waiting for me on the deck. I slowly walked through my yard and up the deck stairs to our second story deck. She greeted me with a sad smile.

"Your father is out with a colleague," she said, "You don't have to hide out there anymore tonight. He'll be home late, most likely after you are in bed."

"Thanks," I said.

Mom hugged me. I smelt a faint scent of a burnt herb she was going to claim as sage from the blanket she wrapped around herself. I went to bed relaxed for once with the memory of Joey's touch soothing me to sleep.

My father, Mitchel Portwood, always thought he was destined for greatness. At the top of his class at his private school in Vermont, he was Ivy League bound. I don't know the particulars of how he wound up going to school in Pittsburg. I don't know how he ended up in Minnesota and met my mother, Patti. For whatever reason, he got a position teaching English at Nicollet Community College, a job he thought was beneath him. All I knew was that he wanted me to meet standards he couldn't reach himself.

Every day he drove me to school. I always missed the bus because I never could find the motivation to get up. Despite keeping my hair short and not wearing makeup, it still took me forever to get ready. My morning ritual consisted of rolling out of bed a half hour after my alarm and standing underneath the warm rain from the shower head for forty minutes. By the time I got dressed and grabbed a granola bar for breakfast, Dad finished his cup of coffee he intended to take to work.

My dad's habit was to wait until we left the neighborhood before he started his morning conversation.

"How long were you walking yesterday?"

"Mom called me in before dark."

Dad drew in a breath. "I was thinking that you need to consider relocating your time. You were out too long last night. You could have researched colleges. You need to start applying this summer. Better yet, you could have spent more time practicing equations. Your math grades were low."

"I am the only student taking three math classes this year," I groaned. "Besides, Mom says I need to balance my time between being in nature and being indoors."

"Your mother is going through a phase," My dad replied, referring to her recent dabbling in marijuana and earth mother lifestyle. She rejected mainstream academia.

"Seems she is enjoying it," I muttered as I closed my eyes and leaned my head against the cold glass of the passenger door.

"It's a midlife crisis she'll soon snap out of," Dad snapped. "When she does, she'll be riding you harder than I am. You better get your act together. This next year is crucial if you want to have any future."

My voice echoed in my brain, *I don't have much of a past, nor a present.*

Dad dropped me off feeling vindicated with the last audible word.

I always floated through the school halls. I tuned everyone out and walk on autopilot. It was how I survived. I didn't begrudge my fellow student's ability to navigate the social landscape to find acceptance. I just didn't see the necessity in being reminded what I lacked. Just attending class and sitting near Erin Barnhart at study hall and lunch were the necessary social function I needed to assume normalcy at school.

I attended Advanced English in the morning then headed towards the library for my free period. I nodded to Erin and sat at the desk next to her. I pulled out my Trigonometry book out of my backpack and began to do problems.

"Boo," whispered the lips against my ear.

I turned around to find Joey standing behind me wearing his lettermen's jacket.

"I figured I'd find you here," he said.

"Aren't you supposed to be in class?" I asked. "I thought your free period was third."

"I have gym. We are lifting weights today, and I lifted yesterday. You have to do it every other day to give your muscles time to build. So, I am free. Come on."

Joey grabbed my hand and yanked me from my chair. Erin looked at me side-eyed. Joey grabbed my book and bag with his other hand. He walked me out of the library.

"Where are we going?"

"To your locker to get your coat."

"Why?"

"It's still cold outside."

"Outside? I can't go outside! I don't have senior privilege."

"It won't matter. I know Tito."

Joy led me down the stairs to my locker. At his direction, I took out my coat and replaced it with my bag. Joey lead me to the back door where the security guard was. It was a rule that if you crossed a guard's path without presented your privilege card, you got sent to detention. Joey opened the door and saluted the guard.

"Hey, Tito!"

"Go ahead, Joey."

Joey saluted the guard and walked me off of the school's lawn.

"Where are we going?"

"Maplewood Park."

"I can't be off campus!"

"We'll go back through the same door we went in. Tito isn't a narc."

"It's his job!"

"He doesn't snitch on me," Joey replied. "I treat him like he is human. None of the other punks do."

The brisk air bit my ear as Joey ran with me to the park. I forgot my hat in my bookbag. Joey ran fast enough to fly me like a kite against the brisk wind. Finally, he had leaned me up against the first tree in the park.

"Joey, why are we here?"

"So, I can do this."

Joey leaned in and kissed me. "We can't do this in school. School policy says it is sexual harassment." As he moved into my neck, he muttered, "And no dark corner is safe from hall monitors. I tried them all."

Joey moved up to my mouth. At first, I was numb to the wind whipping at our bodies. After the minute, the stray saliva on my cheeks started causing them to chap. I buried my head in his chest. He clutched me. I breathed him in.

"Sorry, I got carried away," he said out of breath. "Good thing we stopped. I want to ask you a question."

"Mmm-hmm."

"Will you go to prom with me?"

I broke from the embrace. "What?"

"Yeah, the prom's Friday night and I want you to go with me."

I leaned back against the tree. Prom: The archaic tradition that perpetuated everything wrong with high school? Popular girls being crown queen. Everyone parading themselves and their dates to prove they aren't total losers, why would Joey ask me to go to prom?

"Is that why you've been so, uh, nice?"

"Nice? Aren't I always nice to you?"

"Yes, but today and yesterday you've been very nice."

Joey arched his eyebrows. Then he gave me his crooked grin.

"Well, yesterday was the first day I realized that we are on the same page."

"Apparently not," I said. "Otherwise, you wouldn't ask."

"Seriously, you won't go?"

"It's not my thing."

Joey pushed himself off the tree. I watched him as he paced while running his fingers through his black hair. Then he grabbed his chin and shook his head.

"You know, I am friends with a lot of girls who claim prom is lame. You know what happens? They get asked, and they go. Seriously, who passes up a chance to dress pretty and spend the night pressed up against the guy they like?"

"Lesbians," I answered. "The school hasn't accepted gays. They should. It's the nineties."

Joey walked up to me with his hands in his pocket.

"This is also the year I graduate. Prom is the last party where I have the chance to hang out with all my friends. I mean it, all of my friends. It won't be that way if you don't come with me."

"You didn't care if I was there any other dance you went to," I pointed out. "Anyways you were dating Amber Logans last week. You bought the tickets for her."

"And now we broke up because she was cheating on me with the star baseball player," Joey said exasperatedly. "To tell you the truth, I am not that broken up about it. I'm happy that it happened. I now have a chance with you, or so I thought after last night."

Even after I let him in my pants last night, I didn't dare consider myself Joey's girlfriend. He had the reputation of being the kindest player in our school, but a player none the less. I loved him as my friend. Still, I needed to be realistic in how I viewed my relationships. Apparently, Joey had his own ideas. He walked up to the tree placing one hand on the trunk.

"It's cool that you accept gays. I mean it. Love is love. People shouldn't judge. It's just not cool that you don't think an athlete can go to prom with a smart girl."

I turned to face him. As he arched his eyebrow over his dark eyes, I turned away. Joey inched closer to me.

"What are you scared of?" he whispered as he cupped my breast. "I swear on this tree where I hold your boob; there will be no pigs' blood."

"Pig's blood?"

I jumped away. Joey steadied himself on the tree. I stood and watched him laugh into the trunk. Slowly, he moved towards me until his body was against mine. He wrapped his arms around my waist.

"The only one touching you at prom will be me. I will hold you like this all night. Doesn't that sound nice?"

"It does," I answered. "But it doesn't change the fact that prom is Friday and today is Wednesday. I don't have a dress. I don't have money to buy one. My parents won't give the money. They probably won't let me go."

"You're a smart girl, Marion. You'll find a way, that's if you want to go."

I didn't want to tell Joey he was right. I said I didn't like proms because the truth of the matter was I knew I'd never be asked. As Joey hugged me tighter, I realized I did want a night pressed up against his body, not just second period.

"Give me a day, okay?"

Joey nodded. "Sure. Come on. We got to get going."

Joey walked me back to school, nodding to Tito as we entered the building. He waited as I put my coat back in my locker

"Which class is next?" he asked, "I'll walk you."

"Trigonometry on the second floor."

We walked down the halls. As we passed a couple of Goth girls, Joey stopped.

"Hey, do any of you have black eyeliner? I need something to write with."

A girl with a black bob and black lipstick pulled a marker out of her bag.

"I have a Sharpie."

"Thanks," Joey replied. "I'll give it back to you in a second."

Joey pulled the sleeve of my sweater up my arm. Quickly, he scrawled seven numbers before handing it back to the Goth girl.

"That's my pager number. You call it to get a hold of me."

"I know what pagers are for," I said

"Good. Call it."

Joey walked with me until a friend called his name. I continued despite him telling me to wait. All this was too much to process. I pointed to my arm with the promise to call him. I was young. I naïvely thought I'd had many opportunities to walk with him.

Dinner at the Portwood house made memories of awkward conversations. My mother talked jovially. My father gave brief stoic replies. I remained silent until called upon. The night of Joey's invitation was no exception. Over pork and potatoes, my mother tried to make weekend plans.

"The Minnesota Orchestra is performing Vivaldi's Four Seasons this weekend. I thought we could go. Marion, you love Vivaldi."

"Yep."

My father sighed. "The college's spring production starts this weekend, Patti. I told you that."

"Oh yes, you are putting on 'Taming of the Shrew'. I love Taming of the Shrew. Marion and I will go see it and support you."

"If I want Marion to be exposed to Shakespeare's misogynistic views, we should wait until it is at the Guthrie where professionals perform rather than students checking off acting from their bucket list. If there is something Marion ought to be doing this weekend, it is to focus on her school work than dallying at the theater. I should be able to entrust you with seeing to that she completes her assignments."

Mom's tone sharpened in defeat. "I will."

"Speaking of which, I have to get going," my dad said, "I'm afraid I'll be out late tonight. Production is a mess."

Dad left without saying goodbye. Mom snorted. "What he doesn't want you to see is how he tamed me. I wonder which ingénue will keep him out late."

My parents never wanted me to grow up, yet they always felt I was mature enough to overhear their marital problems. Another thing I never understood about my dad. At forty-eight, my mother was beautiful for her age. She kept her hair blond and long. She never resorted to embroidered sweatshirts. Plus, she had a whimsical air about life. She found the bright side to everything even before she started toking weed.

Mom got up from the table. "Help me clean," she whispered.

I took the plates from the dining nook to our kitchen counter. Mother attempted to hum a happy tune as she put the dishes in the washer, but it came out in a minor key.

"Mom, can I talk to you about Friday?" I asked.

"Hmm-hmm," she answered.

"I got asked to Prom on Friday and..."

Mother turned around clasping her hands over her chest.

"To prom? Really, Marion?"

"Yes. Joey Troli asked me."

"Ah, that kid you've played with in the woods. He asked you this late?"

"He broke up with his girlfriend," I said trying to sound nonchalant. "Anyways, it's not my thing, but I feel sorry for him, so I said I'll go even though I didn't ask you or dad if I could."

"We won't tell your father. Call him and say he has to pick you up before four thirty on Friday."

"What?"

Mother handed me the cordless phone from the wall charger.

"Call him now and make that clear to him. If he comes any later, your father will stop you from going. You can take the phone to your room. Just be quick. The mall closes in two hours."

"The mall?"

" We need to get you a dress and shoes to match. Thankfully, your hair is short because there is no way we can get a hair appointment now. We'll start at Southdale Mall. You can always find something fine at Dayton's. Just hurry up."

I dashed to my room and dialed Joey's pager. After a series of beeps, I dialed my number. Two minutes later the phone rang.

"Portwood residence."

"Good, it's you," Joey answered.

"I can go. You just need to pick me up before four thirty."

"That's a little early."

"If my dad gets home, I can't go."

"Ah, discord between Mommy and Daddy Portwood, eh? Bad for them, but it works in our favor."

"Yeah," I said dryly.

"I was about to go for a walk. Why don't you join me?"

"I can't. Mom is buying me a dress."

"Cool, meet you at your locker tomorrow."

"Yeah, bye."

Mom knocked on the door, rushing me out. Had I known prom was going to be my most special day, I would have savor all the silk and taffeta I endured that night. My wedding to Irving pales in comparison. Only one man made me feel like a princess. My Joey, who I lost all over again.

3

Irving and my father have a habit of talking about me rather than talking to me. In the hospital room, I keep my eyes closed, so they think I am asleep. That is when their conversation gets interesting.

First, it begins with Irving thanking my dad for something, maybe a cup of cafeteria coffee or a pen to fill out my intake forms. My father sighs. I can hear him shift in plastic upholstered chair.

"I went to the psychiatric ward," My father says, "to see about preemptive admittance."

"Why?"

"She attempted suicide three times," my father answers.

"When she was a teenager," Irving recalls.

"Now that she has lost her only chance for a child, she may reconsider her path to mental health," my father remarked. "Seriously, how did you think she was fit to have a kid?"

"I didn't know she went off the pill," Irving defends himself.

I snorted. Before we connected four months ago, I experienced a four-year long sexual drought. Since you had to have sex to get pregnant, I didn't see the need to pay a monthly thirty dollar co-pay. I was able to fund a weekly Caribou Coffee habit with the extra money. I didn't foresee the two of us getting tipsy at the Orchestra banquet. Actually, I was tipsy. Irving was too drunk to remember I was his wife.

"Is all this amusing to you, Marion?" My father asked.

I turn to my other side, which I quickly regret. I heard the force of the accident pushed me against the seatbelt in a diagonal direction hitting where my spine met my hip. I yelp in pain.

"The painkillers were working until this moment," I answer.

"This is a serious matter, Marion," My father remarks.

"Really?" I asked sarcastically. With my baby girl voice, it comes out cutesy instead of chafing.

"Marion, please my dear," Irving pleads.

"Considering I am laying in a hospital bed no longer pregnant, I get the seriousness of the situation. I get it more so than the two of you."

"But you are not in a reasonable frame of mind," my father advises. "Come, Irving, it would be best to have this conversation in the hall."

Irving complies. Before he left the room, he shoots me a loving look. Unfortunately, it's a look one would give to a sister rather than a wife. He goes to discuss my future with my father. They will tell me what they decided. I will comply. I am accustomed to this arrangement.

Irving and my dad leave for the night. Neither of them has taken time off from work. The hospital is to care for me. The doctor mentioned that I would be out in a day, pending my occupational therapy evaluation tomorrow.

A nurse comes in with a wheelchair.

"Ms. Palavar, I am here to take you to your psych evaluation?"

I am not the type of person to question these things. If I fight it, I will end up in the sterile room devoid of life for three days. I never understood why they put those who attempted suicide in a room that perpetuates the inclination. I just need to do what I am told to avoid the ward.

The nurse picks me up and rolls me to a meeting room. Inside is a man with black hair and pale skins. He looks at me with piercing blue eyes. With a blue cardigan and hair slicked, he looks like he came from the roaring twenties.

"You must be Marion Palavar. I am Dr. Joseph Kroll."

A Joey? Is this a sign? A cosmic joke? The wound of my best friend torn open when I saw him in heaven. Now a man bearing the same name will decide my fate?

"Nice to meet you, Joey?"

"It's Joseph," he corrected. "I prefer you call me Dr. Kroll. It maintains professional boundaries."

"Very well, Dr. Kroll."

Dr. Krolls scribbles in a folder. I look around. I am grateful we are in a room with a picture hanging on the wall. It's just a generic floral landscape; but, the fact that it is there means they don't have a fear I will pull it from the wall and throw it across the room like a crazy person. There is a picture window too. I can see the headlights driving pass the Minneapolis Crosstown highway from the window. If the doctors were positive I'm suicidal, I wouldn't be near the sixth floor window.

"You were in a head-on collision. Another car attempted to exit onto the freeway on the wrong ramp."

I nodded. Frankly, I had no memory of the accident.

"It resulted in a spontaneous abortion. Your father expressed concerns about your mental health because you attempted to take your life three times after the death of a friend."

I nodded. The truth was Joey's death was a factor the first attempt. The other two attempts were to get out of my father's thumb. Dr. Kroll didn't need to know that.

"Well, Marion, how do you feel?"

"I am in pain," I answer.

"Physical? Emotional?"

"Physical."

"Just Physical?"

"I understand it is in a woman's nature to act emotionally. My father has coached me to behave rationally. Suicide was a teenage phase."

Dr. Kroll looked at me with arched eyebrows.

"How do you feel about the loss of your baby?"

"Sad," I answer in monotone.

"Sad?"

"Yes. I lost my child."

"I am confused."

I exhale my held breath. This guy is impossible.

"Listen," I begin, "I lost my child. I am sad. Crying and wailing is not going to bring her back. I know from experience. Just tell my father I will still comply and fall in line. I will act sane as humanly possible."

Dr. Kroll scrawls more notes. I've either said too much or not enough. Either way, I didn't say the right thing.

"I think your father is hasty in seeking admittance for you in the mental health ward," Dr. Kroll remark, "However, I will mandate that you comply to an aftercare plan. I will see you weekly."

"I usually see Dr. Harmon Kettering," I explain.

"Dr. Kettering is retired," Dr. Kroll says, "I've taken some of his case load. I will see you once a week from your discharge."

I sigh. I wasn't fond of Dr. Kettering. I found him misogynistic and boorish. He was the devil I knew. Dr. Kroll was blunt as Dr. Kettering, yet in an eloquent manner. I loathed eloquence. It was a mode for people to hide their true intentions.

Dr. Kroll knocks on the door. The nurse comes in and wheels me out.

"How long is she here for?" He asks.

"One more day at least," says the doctor.

Dr. Kroll nods, and I am wheeled back to my room. The nurse asks if I want a warmed blanket. I nod. It is late. However, in the heated felt cocoon, I find little comfort. Leaving my Joeys behind in heaven has driven a hole in my soul. I lay in the same despair I laid twenty-one years ago.

Unfortunately, I know what the future holds.

4

I never cared about clothes beyond their necessity. At least, that is what I claimed in my youth. When I put the wine colored iridescent gown, I couldn't stop staring at my reflection. I blinked multiple times. Even when the image of my beautiful reflection remained after I opened my eyes, I didn't believe I stared at myself.

We got the dress at a discount in Dayton's formal department on clearance. It was last season's color. The colors for the season were pastels, but my pale complexion didn't fare with light colors. Mother liked to joke our Native American to Anglo ratios manifested opposite from each other. Despite having two blond parents, I inherited the thick black hair of my Dakota Indian grandmother. My mother inherited her tan skin. I envied her elder elegance growing up. I never thought I'd lived up to her beauty; but as she directed ooh's and ahh's at me as I tried on dresses, I got a glimmer of hope I could.

Mom came in with a pearl headband. She placed it on my head.

"I used the band to fashion a headdress for my wedding. Now I gift it to you."

The wedding picture on the mantel shown my mother having daisies woven through her hair. She shook her head as my face contorted in confusion.

"Your Grandmother Portwood didn't approve. Come to think of it, neither did your Grandpa Larson. I glued these big fake white feathers to the band. It was truly a sight. Your father, he wanted a small wedding without much ceremony. We compromised, and I wore the daisies."

Mother stared at me through the mirror.

"You are truly lovely, Marion. I am glad you finally get to have a fun school experience. I had a few pleasant memories of school dances myself. I hate that your focus became purely academic."

She hugged my shoulders when we heard the doorbell ring.

"You're young. You have to have some fun."

Mother ran downstairs and answered the door for Joey. I could only walk in my heels. Mother opened the door revealing Joey smiling in in tan three-piece suit with black shirt and tie. I stopped at the top the stairs. Seeing Joey dressed in his formal attire actualized the reality that I was going to prom. He waved at me then held out a box containing a white rose corsage.

"Marion," Mother urged, "Get down here. I want pictures before you need to leave."

I lifted my full-length skirt an inch, so I could walk without tripping on it. As my mother blinded us with her camera, Joey slipped the corsage on my left wrist. She ushered us outside where she took our pictures near her rose bushes and the shrub hedge. Suddenly she looked at her watch.

"Your father is going to be home any minute. You better be heading out."

Joey walked me to the driveway. Mother stopped short at the sight of the black Cadillac parked in the driveway.

"Is this your car?" she asked.

"No," Joey answered. "My neighbor works for a car rental place. He gave me a discount. My dad had a Cadillac when he was alive. I always wanted to drive one."

Mother lifted her camera. On cue, Joey wrapped his arm around my waist and smiled for the camera. Mother took a couple of pictures until she turned and gasped. A familiar tan sedan turned onto our cul-de-sac.

"Get in the car and drive now!"

Joey entered the driver's seat. Mom opened the back door and pushed me in.

"Worry about buckling up when you are out of harm's way."

I snickered at the irony. Joey had pulled out of the driveway moments before Dad approached it. As our cars passed Joey saluted Dad. I peeked over the backseat as we drove away. Dad stared at us then turned to yell at Mother. Mother turned away from him with a wave of her hand. I slumped down and giggled.

"My mom silently told my dad to 'Talk to the hand.'"

Joey let out a slight chuckle as he drove out of my street.

We pulled up to an apartment complex down the road. Joey opened my car door and picked me up. He carried me across the lawns then through a woodland clearing until I saw a familiar paved path. Joey put me down on the cement.

"This is how you enter Miles Creek?"

"Yes."

Joey pulled out a disposable camera from his pocket then proceed to walk me down the path.

"As you can see, I didn't have that much money to go to prom. All I could afford were the tickets. Well, all my mom could afford. She doesn't let me have a job during the school year, so I am often low on funds. I couldn't afford the photo package; but, I figured you wouldn't mind skipping the part where we stand in front of tulle for an awkward photograph. Instead, let's have the place we love to be our backdrop."

Despite that the trees were still naked, the creek remained the most beautiful place I knew. I took the camera, wrapped Joey's arm around me and took a picture of the two of us.

"Hey, don't waste film!"

"How else are we supposed to get a picture?"

Joey took the camera from my hand. He walked me down the path. We came to the overlook bridge above the pipe of the city's storm sewer. I looked down where the creek flowed under the bridge. The rocky shore did make for a picturesque backdrop. I started heading down to the water. Joey stopped me. He pointed to a runner whose dark ponytail flopped as she ran.

"Maybe she will take our picture."

Joey flagged the runner down the path. She stopped quizzically.

"Hey! Can you take a picture of my girlfriend and me? We are going to prom and hate tulle backdrops!"

The runner ran up to us. She broke into a smile as she reached for the camera.

"Lucky for you, I am a photographer who hates tulle backdrops. I see what I can do with what we have. I'll first have you move to the left to reduce the sun's glare."

Joey and I complied with the directives. We had five pictures overlooking the creek. She moved us closer to the woods and took five more pictures. One picture she swore a deer came into view behind us. The woman dared us to walk on to the rock.

"She will get her dress wet!" Joey protested.

I lifted my skirt and ran to the edge. Joey had caught me before I tripped over my foot. The woman laughed as she snapped a picture. As we steadied ourselves, we took four more pictures on the shore of the creek.

"Thank you very much," Joey said, pulling out his wallet. He pulled out a five dollar bill. "For your troubles."

The woman waved her hand. "The pleasure is all mine."

She started running as we went back onto the path.

"Hey," she shouted turning back. "If you haven't taken your senior pictures, you can look me up at Talia's Best In Class Studios. I specialize in Senior Portraits."

"Will do!" Joey shouted back.

We got back to the clearing. Standing at the end, I realized Joey carried me down an incline. I couldn't expect him to take me while climbing a hill. Not to be deterred, Joey bent down.

"Climb on my back."

"Are you crazy?"

Joey backed into me and pinned my legs against him from behind. He stood up.

"If you'd seen me wrestle, I can pop a guy twice my size off my back. Giving you a piggy back ride up a hill will be nothing. Although, if you intend to break my heart tonight, let me know now. That way I can toss you in the mud."

Joey bounced me on his back until I yelped. I wrapped my arms around his neck, but he loosened them. He moved them down to his shoulders. I pulled him into a tighter embrace.

"That's better," he said.

I rested on Joey as he carried me to his car. "This is the way to travel," I said.

Joey put me down next to the car and opened the door for me. We entered the car. As Joey buckled his seatbelt, I asked, "What was with you telling the photographer that I was your girlfriend?"

Joey turned his head, "You don't want to be?"

"No, I do."

Joey leaned over to me and kissed my lips.

"Then you are."

Because I loved Joey since we were children, the simple kiss was all the sweet declaration I needed.

Prom was held at The International Market Square in Minneapolis. It was just a building with a grand lobby. White Christmas lights wrapped around the hall's pillars. The dance floor was set in the foyer with the tables placed in the hallways around it. After the grand march, Joey tried to find a small table for us to sit.

"Hey, Troli! You're looking for us!"

"Damn," Joey whispered, "Chauncey spotted us. We have to go sit with him and Amber is at his table."

"Maybe we can act like there isn't enough room when we get to the table," I whispered, "That way we don't seem rude."

As Joey and I walked over, Chauncey pulled out two chairs.

"I don't think we will be as lucky," Joey muttered.

Luckily I was a mastered of smiling through awkward situations. Well, even today I am great at faking a genuine smile. Joey leading me to the table that day wasn't the worst. Months later, I'd be smiling through my unending mouring.

Joey and Chauncey did some team handshake that ended with a half hug. Joey then wrapped his arm around me. "You all know, Marion?"

Everyone shook their head.

"Everyone, Marion," Joey replied, "Marion, this is everyone."

"What my esteem friend means," Chauncey remarked, "Is that everyone has a name. We are Chauncey, Kayla, Matthew, Sarah, Mike, and Amber."

"Esteemed friend?" Joey replied as he took his seat.

Chauncey muttered, "Whatever, man?"

We sat through dinner listening to the other girls converse amongst themselves. I politely smiled when called upon. Thankfully we didn't have to endure our entire dinner of catered chicken, salad, and strawberry cheesecake. The moment the music came on Joey swept me up and carried me to the dance floor. Eric Clapton's "Wonderful Tonight" played. Joey held me tight as we swayed to the music.

"I told you this wouldn't be so bad," Joey whispered.

"Now that you are holding me as close as promised," I replied.

"I'm not letting you go," Joey said, "It's you and me without an inch between us the entire night."

"Promise?"

"Promise."

Joey kept his promise as the rest of his class started jumping to House of Pain. Even when everyone moshed to Green Day's "Basket Case." Chauncey tried to jump in between us during Beastie Boys' "Fight for Your Right to Party," to no avail.

"Chauncey," Joey said as he shook his head, "He always has to be the clown of the party. I like the guy, but his antics gets old. Part of me is going to be glad to be away from all of this next year."

"Where are you going to be?" I asked.

"Nicollet."

I looked up at him. "Really? You are staying in town?"
"The trust my grandmother set up for me doesn't kick in until I'm twenty-one. I applied to Nicollet where I can get my associates until I can afford to go to a university. It won't be so bad if you apply to their post-secondary program. Maybe we can take some of the same classes and have lunch every day."

"That 'd be great."

"Yeah, maybe you'll get a chance to be the real Marion next year," Joey said, "not that ghost who floats the hall."

"What does that have to do with anything?"

"At school, I don't recognize you because you walk the halls like a zombie. That is not Marion Portwood I meet in the woods. The Marion I know is full of life. At least she is when she is hiking. Not when she is smoking. You are going to stop smoking, right?"

"As long as you keep kissing me," I answered.

Joey kissed me full and hard. Then the music stopped; it wasn't because of our kiss. Everyone stopped and looked at the DJ booth. A teacher I recognized in passing stood in front of everyone.

"Excuse me," she said. "Is there a Marion Portwood here?"

I didn't know another person from my generation named Marion. Everyone who sat our table looked over at me. Everyone else followed their gaze.

"If there is a Marion Portwood here, you are needed at the front door."

"What the?" Joey exclaimed.

I burrowed myself into his embrace. The teacher lead by the other students' gazes walked over and separated us.

"Your father is here," she whispered.

"What!" yelled Joey.

The teacher took me by the hand and led me to the front door. Joey followed. I heard the music turn on behind us. Still, the other students watched me get escorted to the door. My father stood stonefaced. He murmured a thank you to the teacher then dragged me out. I felt Joey's fingertip as he attempted to grab me. My dad charged out the door.

"What are you doing?" I screamed when we were outside.

"Taking you home!" he yelled, "you didn't have permission to come here!"

"Yeah, I did! Mom gave it to me!"

"Your mother hasn't been in her right mind for a while. It wasn't her place to allow you a break from your studies."

I attempted to pull away. My tiny waif frame was no match for his tight grip. I resigned to my fate as we reached the car.

Father didn't say anything during the car ride. I looked out the window hoping to see Joey driving the Cadillac behind us. It wasn't there. Without an escape in sight, I stewed in my anger. This event was too audacious for my father. Sure he was stern and controlling, but he behaved mild mannered. Most said his controlling nature was a sign he cared about my well-being. Pulling me from the safety of Joey was not an act of love.

Surprisingly, Mother shared my views on the situation. She rose from the couch as we entered the house.

"You didn't!"

Father put out his hand. "I did. End of story. Marion, go to your room."

"Gladly."

"You watch your mouth!"

I slammed my bedroom door as hard as I could. I unzipped my dress and put it on my white desk chair. Catching the reflection of my made up face, I realized I didn't want to wear the usual flannel pajamas. I didn't want to be standard Marion anymore. I couldn't. I was Joey Troli's girlfriend now.

I pulled a box from my bed. It contained my forbidden nightie. I found it years ago amongst the family's donation to Goodwill. I snuck it from the pile and hid it in my room. With the light blue beadwork at the waist, I figured it was my mothers'. Before she married my father, she would make her clothes to reflect her Native American and Swedish heritage. I kept it as proof of my material heritage. That night, I wanted to feel beautiful. I wasn't going back to being standard Marion.

The nightgown hung low at my chest. I didn't have the boobs to fill it out. Still, it was more sophisticated than candy striped pajamas. I dressed and went to bed pulling out my copy of "The Scarlet Letter" from my backpack. I could relate to Hester Prynne's plight now; however, I couldn't pay attention. My parents' voices broke through the barrier of my bedroom door.

"Just let me know what right you have in humiliating her like that?"

"I'm saving her!"

"From what, Mitchell? Friends? A teenage social life?"

I heard my father stomp up the stairs. He must have been heading out the door when my mother yelled at him.

"She needs to focus on what's important! She has potential! She isn't reaching!"

"Reaching what? You set your standards so high you can't even see that they aren't attainable. She is still a bright kid none the less."

"She is ranked one hundredth in her class."

"Out of one thousand. She is still in the top ten percent."

"She needs to be at the top! She could if you have her focus! Instead, the moment I leave for the night, you let her traipse in the woods with that boy!"

"That boy is Joey. They have been friends since they were kids!"

"He is only at 275 in his class, and it only has 956 students! She can do better."

"How do you know his class ranking?"

I got out of bed and pushed my ear against the door. How did Dad get Joey's school records?

"He's applied to Nicollet! He's going to a community college! She could go to an Ivy League school if she can push herself, but she is settling for a community college!"

"You call the records office on him?" Mother asked. "Do you know how pathetic you are? Truly, do you want Marion to be the next Emily Dickenson? By that, do you just want her to be a pathetic loner? I had friends when I was a kid. I still made it to grad school. I met you there!"

"Yes, despite you being a hippie junkie, you made something of yourself. But Marion will do better. She can accomplish more than teaching worthless trailer trash and…"

"Burnt out Native Americans?" Mother finished. "You've said it before. Get your racist ass out of my sight and go bed your latest ingénue while you can."

I heard Mom's slipper covered feet walk off the steps.

"Patti, wait!" Dad called out. "That wasn't a racist slur. You're white more than you are Dakota and I wish you would stop taking what I say as derogatory."

"Well, this mostly white ass lost her virginity at sixteen. You lost yours at the age of twenty at a brothel in Montreal. Now, you do your students to make up for lost time? You're the reason I smoke weed. The fact that I am married to you sickens me. Now go."

I heard the door slam. I ran to the bed and turned off my light. Mom may be on my side, but I didn't want to have a conversation about my parents' marriage. It turned to a conversation about their sex life. Even if we were close, I never wanted to know my parents' intimate details.

Children at any age should live in blissful ignorance in that regard.

The moment the smell of sweetgrass filled the house, I got out of bed. I put on my leather coat and sneakers. Searching the pantry, I found the flashlight. I made sure that the door closed quietly not to disturbed my mother. I didn't turn it on until I passed the hedges.

Despite never walking into the woods at night before, I knew the trail habitually. At least muscle memory could get me to the fort. I would have to guess which forks in the trail could take me to Joey's apartment.

When I got to the fort, I saw it lit up from inside. I started walking up the hill.

"Joey?"

Joey's face appeared.

"Marion?"

I put the flashlight against my face then waved. Joey exited the fort. He's changed into jeans, but his black dress shirt and tie were still on.

"Wow!" Joey exclaimed, "Look at you! Um, you're early. Do you mind waiting down there for a moment?"

"For what?"

"It is still prom night," Joey shouted out as he disappeared into the fort.

I watched Joey's shadow shuffle around the fort. The cold wind rustled around the bottom of my gown. Cinching at the side didn't deter it from going up my gown. Now I wished I'd put on underwear before going outside.

Joey walked down the hill scattering white rose petals. As he reached me, he flung a handful up in the air then grab me for a kiss. After the petals fell on us, he led me up the trail of rose petals to the fort. Joey shone the flashlight into the fort. Pillow, sheets, and blankets flung around made it look like a royal harem. Red rose petals scattered over a white sheet. I turned to kiss Joey on the cheek. He fingered the buttons on my coat.

"May I?"

I nodded. Joey took off my coat revealing the nightgown. He sighed and started kissing my neck.

"Since when do you walk in the woods dressed like that?"

"I was looking for you."

"Yeah," Joey said as he breathed me in. "Good thing I was waiting for you."

"Really?"

Joey came up from my neck. " My plan was to walk to your house and find your window. I was going to do the cliché throw stones until you open your window. I'd convince you to come outside and lead you here. I didn't want tonight to end with you being escorted away from the dance. I wanted to be memorable in a meaningful way; at least I hope."

Joey steadied me into the fort laying down against the pillows and sheets. He started to light votive candles around the entrance and turned off the flashlight.

"Aren't you afraid of setting the woods on fire?" I joked.

Joey laid on top of me. "I intend to be very careful."

Joey kissed me softly. His kisses turn passionate. Soon, his hand pushed the bottom of my gown up. He gasped when he felt the bare skin on my bottom.

"Are you okay?" I asked.

"Yeah, I just…."

"You just what?"

Joey bent back down to kiss me.

"I've wanted you, Marion. I've wanted you for a long time. From your lack of particular garments, I guess you feel the same way. May I?"

"You've got…"

Joey pulled out a line of condoms.

"You may," I said.

Joey took off his pants. I bit my lip as I watch him put his condom on. I knew Joey figured I was a virgin; still, I didn't want to be obvious by gasping at his manhood. He slid into me and gently moved inside me. A minute later he finished by cursing.

"Sorry, I usually last longer…"

I pulled his tie and lowered his face to mine. We kissed then he laid down next to me. We spent the night alternating between sleeping and making love. Sometime during the evening, he asked me, "What's your middle name?"

"My middle name?"

"Yes, I've known you for seven years and never knew your middle name. Now that you are my girlfriend and we went all the way, we ought to know each other's middle names."

"What's yours?"

"I asked you first," Joey said.

"It's Shire," I groaned.

"Shire?"

"Where the hobbits lived in 'The Lord of The Rings.' It is my father's favorite book. My mother put her foot down when he tried naming me Arwen. My mother wanted my name to be Robin after Robin Hood, but my father didn't want me to have a boy's name."

Joey shrugged, "All the Robins I know are girls."

"They compromised, and I became Marion Shire Portwood. Now you."

"My full name is Joseph Stallone Troli. Joseph is my grandfather's name. Sylvester Stallone was my father's hero. His favorite movie was 'Rocky.' He wanted to call me Rocky, but my grandfather told my dad the only way he was going to let him marry his daughter was if he named his son after him. My parents compromised too."

"Joseph Stallone. The name suits you."

The condoms were gone by the time the sun started to rise. The candles long flickered out. Joey handed me my coat and wrapped a blanket over me.

"I'll walk you home."

We walked to my hedge border. I kissed Joey.

"Don't you want me to walk you to your door?"

"I'll be okay."

Joey embraced me. "What are the chances you will escape the house the rest of the weekend?"

"Absolutely none."

"Then I am excited about school on Monday."

Joey kissed me hard. I watch him head back into the woods. Once he was gone, I headed up the deck. My father sat at the kitchen table with his coffee and newspaper. I glided over to my room ohoping he was engrossed in The Minneapolis Star Tribune. No such luck.

"Marion? Were you out all night!"

I quickly escaped to my bedroom. Once in bed, I wrapped Joey's blanket tightly around me. I heard the clamor of my father's accusations about negligent parenting to my mother. I was too tire to listen. I fell asleep smiling.

5

My father gifted us the house when Irving and I got married. We didn't do much to alter the place. Walking into it from the hospital is different now. The air of the excitement from a pending change is gone. Returning to fill the void is oppressive stagnation along with a mournful fog.

Irving walks me up the stairs to the common area of the upper spilt-level. He steadies me on the couch. I lay down and close my eyes.

"Can I get you anything, Dear?"

"How about a bottle of hard cider that we bought from Vermont?"

"You are on Vicodin," Irving scolds.

"I am not operating heavy machinery," I reply.

"I'll make you tea. Would herbal mint be alright?"

"It will be fine," I concede.

Irving walks to the kitchen. I close my eye. I pretend the bustling in the kitchen is Joey fixing me tea. I imagine him standing in front of the microwave with the beard as I saw him in heaven. Hearing the microwave go off I squint my eyes. Without the hard cider, I cannot believe that little Irving with his light thinning hair is tall, dark Joey.

Irving hands me my tea. I barely can squeak out a thank you. Irving goes back into the kitchen. He was never one to hang around when I needed someone to care for me. It doesn't matter. He is not who I ever needed.

"Dr. Wester called today. She is going to email me the FML papers."

"There is no baby," I groaned, "what do we need the Family Medical Leave Act for?"

"You were in a traumatic accident, Marion. Your bones may have only chipped, but recovery is going to take some time. As an administrator, you are allowed only six days of sick time. It will take longer for you to recover."

"I'll be fine," I groan, "I'll just take the Vicodin."

Irving pokes his head from the side of the wall that separates the kitchen from the common area.

"Those pills are addictive," he lectures. "You will have to watch your intake. You will avoid alcohol until your prescription runs out. Good thing we carpool to work because you can't be driving."

"Good thing everything is delivered," I say.

Irving walks into the common area. With closed eyes, I can tell he is carrying a bottle of hard cider by the smell of it. He sits on the arm of the couch near my feet. He is trying to play devoted husband. The truth is the success of our marriage is because I don't expect Irving to be present. Our marriage was a means to the end of my father's entrapment of my life. It is in these moments where he makes a conscious effort to be a loving husband that are the most awkward.

"Do you have a class to prepare for?" I ask.

"Yes. Yes, I do."

"It would be more productive of you to prepare instead of watching me laying here, groaning."

"But if you need anything, I ought to get it for you."

I force a sweet smile. "All I need is to rest. You don't need to watch me sleep."

"Very well."

Irving retreats to the study that was once my mother's former sanctuary. I hear the Disney-like sounds of Gustav Mahler barely escaping the door. Knowing Irving is off in his own world, I lift myself up from the couch by pushing my torso up with my elbows. The Vicodin subsides the pain enough to allow me to get up, but not without labor.

I walk to the refrigerator and grab the last bottle of hard cider before limping to the French doors that exit onto the deck. Pulling the sheer curtains away, I look out to the backyard. The hedge border is gone. Father ripped it out after my first suicide attempt. After losing Joey, I tried drowning myself in the creek. He replaced the hedge with a gateless seven-foot wooden fence. Being banned from the creek inspired an overdosed of pills. Then Father took away my freedom by having me claimed as a vulnerable adult. I tried killing myself to achieve freedom. My mistake was slicing them in front of Dad at the dinner table. It was my failed statement to declare he was truly the one who was killing me. I'm still not allowed to touch knives.

I look outside, and all I see is gray. The trees are naked. Joey is not emerging from the trees. He is not walking through the fence. I go back to lay down.

My mother often spoke of our ancestors communicating with spirits in altered states. That was her claim for smoking marijuana. With Vicodin and alcohol in my system, I think I should see Joey any moment. I don't see the high school wrestler kissing my head. Nor do I see the rugged wilderness man he became in heaven. I can't smell the clean sugar air. Not that I should. No one should me rewarded for poisoning themselves.

Still, I lay down and close my eyes. I pretend a draft against my face is Joey's light kiss. I roll over against the back cushions to deluding myself to think I lay against Joey's body. I wish I was in heaven again.

6

Prom made me an unlikely celebrity of Bloomington's John F. Kenney High School. The moment I entered the door, people popped up in front of my face.

"You're THAT girl from prom!"

"That had to be so embarrassing!"

"Yeah," I answered slinging my bag over my shoulder, "but it's cool."

"Cool? Your dad ruined your prom night."

"Yeah, but my date saved it," I replied.

Amber appeared in earshot. "Yeah, I bet he did."

An arm wrapped around my shoulders. "Ms. Portwood is done taking your questions!"

I looked up to my beloved Joey's smile. He kissed my cheek.

"Consider me your escort to all of your classes today," he said.

"Thank you."

As we walked to my English class, Joey bent down and whispered, "I had nothing to do yesterday but lift weights. I am skipping second period and you, my dear, will accompany me to the park."

"I'll skip Trigonometry," I whispered, "I am never going to understand it. Think of all the time we can spend at the park."

"If you are skipping Trig, we can take a longer walk."

The longer walk ended up being the half an hour walk to Miles Creek. Joey led me to our fort. No sooner did we reach it, he started kissing me and lowering me inside it. A sheet from prom night remained on the ground with the crumpled rose petals. After a minute of kissing my neck and grabbing my chest, Joey pulled a condom from his pocket.

"You carry those around all the time?"

"I want to seize every opportunity I have with you," Joey said as he pulled down our pants. "The past two days have been torture. I think about you all the time."

Joey made love to me strong yet tenderly. When we climaxed, he fell on top of me. I clutched him close to my bosom, wishing for a way to get closer than humanly possible.

"One of these days I am going to get you in a proper bed," Joey said, "nothing but skin to skin."

"I'd like that."

"How long until Daddy Portwood loosens the reins?"

"A long awhile and the sudden grade drop in trigonometry that will occur this week won't help."

"How do you know your grade is going to drop?"

"Because you are going to lift weights at home and skip the gym for me," I said kissing him, "and I'll skip trigonometry for you. And we'll come here."

Joey kissed me. "I want to take you on a real date, Marion, dinner, a movie, sneaking you into my apartment and fool around in my bed."

"Patience," I hushed. "He'll let up eventually. Fridays he always goes out, and my mother is preoccupied. You can take me out then."

Joey's watched started beeping. He hugged me.

"I hate to say it, but we have to put our pants on and head back to school."

I sighed but complied. My dad was picking me up from school versus having me take the bus. If I weren't at the front of the school, I'd get grounded until graduation. Before we left the fort, I kissed Joey long and hard. He had to move me down the path.

We continued the same sequence each day. That was my favorite week of school. The routine unraveled on Friday night.

Dad didn't leave until late that Friday. We spent the entire evening with him bearing down on me about my paper on "King Lear." Despite reading the tragedy, I wouldn't have minded a dutiful sibling to seize my father's attention if it freed me from his scrutiny.

Mother brought home Chinese food, and we ate silently at the table. By the time the last piece of Sweet and Sour chicken got plunked from the carton, both my parents got up and carried out their night. I waited until I heard Dad close the garage door before I paged Joey.

I waited fifteen minutes, but Joey didn't call. He typically called me the second I paged. I dialed and waited five minutes. I walked to the porch door. Despite seeing thunder from a distance, I decided to go into the woods. I found Joey there the week before. Maybe he was setting up another date.

Lightning started to strike when I crossed the Miles Creek path. Suddenly the rain started. I sprinted to the fort. I could see the light emitting from inside. The rain made the hill slippery with mud. I carefully climbed until I reached our sanctuary, unable to believe what I saw.

Illuminated by the flashlight he held, Joey sat inside crying. I touched his shoulder. He jumped startled.

"Jesus Christ, Marion! What are you doing here?"

"I was looking for you. Joey, what's wrong?"

"Nothing."

"You don't cry over nothing."

"How do you know?"

I sat down next to him.

"The last time I saw you cry was when we found a dead fawn in the creek. Remember the summer the river flooded? You pressed your face hard into a tree so I wouldn't notice. You ended up having total bark face."

Joey shrugged. I wrapped my arm around him.

"Tell me what happened."

"I'm homeless. That is what's happening!"

"What?" I screamed.

Joey choked on his sobs. "The asshole my mother married kicked me out! She let him!"

"Why?"

"Nothing. He went to play poker. My mother saw I was still home tonight and told me she was taking me out to eat. We went to Sidney's at the Galleria then she wanted to see some chick flick. She dragged me to the movies. We come home, and the asshole is mad that she wasn't there to serve his dinner. He tried to jump her. I jumped him. He told me to leave and never come back. I looked at her…she just tells me to leave…not to make trouble."

Joey punched the ground.

"She chose the asshole that wanted to beat her up over me! Her son! The one who protects her!"

Joey put his head against his knees and sobbed. I held him tighter despite his body shaking. The raindrops turned into sheets. In an instant we were soaked. When the thunder drummed steadily, I knew we had to leave.

"Come with me," I said. "I am taking you to my house."

"I got to figure out where I am going."

"Here? In the rain?"

"It's the only place I have right now!"

"I have a bed at my house," I whispered. "We can fool around skin to skin like you wanted."

Joey shook his head at me. "My mother abandoned me. You think that sex is what is on my mind right? I'm homeless."

I sighed. "I'm just trying to say anything to convince you to get out of the rain."

Rain poured into the fort. Our soaking clothes stuck to our skin.

"You better go home," Joey said.

"No."

"Don't be dumb, Marion. You'll catch your death sitting in this."

"So will you."

"Marion! Just go home where you'll be safe."

I snorted. "Safe? You are going to sit here in the rain while I walk home alone. That is not exactly 'safe,' Joey."

"Just do what I tell you so I can have peace of mind."

"Joey, do you think I am going to leave my homeless boyfriend alone in the rain? You don't think that highly of me if that is the case. I am going to sit here as long you are here."

"Go home."

"Come with me."
"How am I going to get through the door without getting you into

trouble?"

"Easy," I said standing up. "It's getting you out that will be harder. Come on."

I pulled on Joey's arm. He sat there obstinately. I tugged harder. Once he realized my willingness to pull his arm out of his socket, he stood up. With his hand in mine, I lead him to my house. The driving rain made it hard to see beyond five feet in front of us. Thankfully, I turned on the porch light before I left. It guided us home.

I opened the door and peered inside. Nobody was in the common areas. I motioned for Joey to follow me to my room, ignoring him as he loudly sniffed the smoke coming from Mom's office. Once I shut the door behind us, he asked, "It's that..."

"Sweetgrass," I answered. "My mother is part Dakota. It is a holy herb."

"Sweetgrass is another word for marijuana. I dumped girls over that stuff."

"I don't use it."

"Still, your mother smokes it? How does she get it? I can't be around that stuff. If it were still wrestling season, I would get kicked off the team."

"I don't think you should be criticizing anybody else's parents right now," I said going through my closet. "But if you must, criticize my dad. He drives her insane as well. Sweet grass is her coping mechanism. Unlike the white man's vice, it is less likely to kill you."

"What are you talking about?"

"Alcohol," I answered, "now let's drop the subject."

"Fine," Joey muttered, "just get me dry."

"I'm working on it."

Joey wrestled in the lightweight class; but, him muscles made his wider than me. He also was half a foot taller. Even my baggiest clothes would be too tight for him. I gave up searching my closet. I was about to go through our laundry for some of my father's clothes. Then I saw my terry cloth bathrobe on my desk chair. I handed it to him.

"Here. Put on this. I'll wash and dry your clothes, so you have something to wear tomorrow. We can walk over to the ARC shop to get you new clothes until we figure something out."

"Am I going to be a prisoner in your bedroom?"

"At least for tonight."

"There are worse places I could be right now," Joey replied as he took off his shirt.

He took everything else off as well. Everything but his Saint Joseph medal. He handed me his wet clothes, but like an idiot, I stood dumbfounded. Joey gave me a smug look.

"It's not like you haven't seen any of this before, Marion."

"I just never saw it all at once," I stammered.

"It's not as impressive when it is limp," Joey said giving his phallus a playful shake.

"It's impressive enough," I squeaked.

"You were going to wash those."

"Yes. Yes, I was."

"Wait a minute."

Joey took his jeans and pulled condoms out of his pocket. He put them on the desk.

"We don't want Daddy Portwood finding these," he said, handing the pants back to me.

"Ah, no," I said.

I walked to the laundry room. Faint sounds of the Moody Blues floated through Mom's study as I passed it. I walked downstairs hoping my mother was too immersed in white satin to notice my scurrying.

Once in the laundry, I threw Joey's clothes in the washer. I took off mine and threw them in with his clothes. In case I forgot to change machines, my parents would think it was simply my load of clothes. The three of us never care to find the time to sit and fold laundry. Anything clean was in two baskets next to the dryer. I rummaged through to find a tank pajama set. Once I put it on, I ran up to my room.

Joey laid on my bed twirling the belt to my light blue bathroom. The yellow terry cloth star patches couldn't even emasculate him. Instead, he chuckled at the sight of my navy pajamas with white stars printed on them.

"Hey, we match."

"My dad isn't home yet," I said. "If you want to brush your teeth, do it now. I got a toothbrush from the dentist the other day. I haven't used it."

"Sure."

We went into the bathroom to brush our teeth. Within seconds of putting the brushes in our mouths, I heard the garage door go up. We quickly spit and ran into the bedroom. I shut off the light.

"Do you have a lock on the door?" Joey asked.

"No. Only my parents' room locks."

Joey grabbed the desk chair and leaned it against the door knob. Placing his hand on the small of my back, he led me to bed. When we pulled the covers over ourselves, Joey wrapped my arm around him and rolled over.

"I never got to be the small spoon," Joey whispered. "It's nice."

I kissed his head. He fell asleep first. I remain awake listening to the sounds of my parents moving around the house. My stomach flipped the moment I heard footsteps neared the door. Thankfully they turned towards the kitchen. Lights flickered out, and the house was quiet and still. I nestled into Joey's back to fall asleep.

We awoke to a loud banging on the door. "Come on, Marion, we have to get going."

Joey rolled over with his eyes wide. I placed my finger to my lips. I moved the chair from the door and walked out acting groggy. My parents stood in the kitchen, both dressed for the day. I squinted as the clock read seventy-thirty.

"It's so early," I whined.

"Of Course it is," Dad commented, "We have to pick up your Grandma Larson in Shakopee, then head over to Red Wing for your cousin's jingle dress exposition."

I forgot this was the weekend of my cousin Keisha's pageant.

"I can't go," I said.

"Marion, why not?" Mom asked.

Suddenly, she stood in front of me. Taking my face in her hands, she gave me a securitizing look.

"Your face is red," she said. "Does your head throb at one side?"

"Yes?"

Mom turned her face towards my father. "She has high blood pressure, Mitch, not that I am surprised."

"Not now, Patty."

Mom kissed my forehead. "You have been pushed to the brink with all those AP classes, haven't you? Stay home and rest. The last thing you need is to be around all the drumming. It will make your head worst. Just go to back to bed."

"If she is staying home, she can work on her Trigonometry homework. Somehow she's behind."

Mom dropped her hands. "I wonder how that is possible," she remarked snidely. "Come on, Mitch."

Mother walked to the stairs of the landing. Dad stammered, "If Marion doesn't have to go, I don't see…"

Mother opened the door to the garage. "We have a deal, Mitch. I go to Vermont on Thanksgiving for a mediocre dinner with your sister, during which I restrain myself as I endure her passive aggressive racist rants. Your end of the bargain is to pretend you appreciate diversity within my family."

Dad walked over to the garage.

"At least one page of your Trigonometry homework. I think you can manage that."

I watched my parents leave the house. As the door closed, I ran to my room. Joey was still in bed, but the robe was on the floor.

"Your parents are gone for the day? How did we get lucky?"

"I am going downstairs to put your clothes in the dryer," I said.

Joey motioned me to the bed. The moment I crawled in, he rolled on top of me. Cupping my chin in his hand, he kissed me. He started rubbing my back.

"It's Saturday morning," He said into my neck. "You're supposed to sleep in on Saturday. May I?"

I nodded. Joey lifted my tank top up. I pulled down my pants as Joey pulled a condom from the pillow he slept on. Until the grandfather clock in the living room chimed noon, we came together, skin to skin. I didn't want the morning to end. Only when confined by Joey's body I felt free.

At last, Joey kissed me and said, "That is all I have in me right now. I got to shower and recharge."

"I'll go put your clothes in the dryer."

Joey headed to the bathroom naked. I put on my robe and headed downstairs to throw our laundry into the dryer.

Joey emerged from the bathroom soaking wet with a towel wrapped around his waist. He hugged and kissed me when I got up the stairs.

"The shower is all yours."

"I just put your clothes in the dryer, but that was, uh, quick."

"I didn't need to take a long one thanks to you," Joey replied. "You don't mind if I place a long distance call on your phone."

"Nope."

"Thanks," said Joey. "Enjoy your shower."

I needed a long shower. I let the water pour down me like a comforting salve of sanity. Because my father wasn't home, I stood in there until my skin wrinkled.

An hour later, I emerged from the bathroom in my robe to reclaim Joey's scent on my skin. Joey sat at my desk at my computer wearing his clothes. He was logged into my American Online account looking at Amtrak fares. Dad had me post my password on my cork board, claiming it was for my safety.

"Hey," he responded as I wrapped my arms around him.

"What are you doing?"

"Seeing that there isn't a train from Minnesota to California," Joey replied.

"California?"

"I called my cousin, Marty, in Anaheim. I told him what happened. My aunt overheard and got on the phone. She demands I live with them if my mother is tossing me out. She has a friend at Amtrak who could comp my ticket. Amtrak only has a track into Washington State. I'm SOL."

"You are not going to California," I replied.

"Why? I have nothing here."

"Joey, you graduate in three weeks! You're going to Nicollet next year."

"Nicollet was contingent on me haven't my rent covered. I don't anymore. My mom never allowed me to have a job, so I have no money for an education."

"But you can't go to California."

"I'll call my aunt and tell her Amtrak is not an option. She'll find some other way to get me to California."

"Fine!"

"Aww, Marion, don't be like that!"

Joey's pager beeped. He peeked at it.

"It's Chauncey."

"Call him," I said, "see if I care."

I went downstairs and pulled some clean clothes from the baskets. I went upstairs to Joey finishing his conversation. He looked at me as I entered the bedroom and said goodbye to Chauncey. I undid my robe and proceeded to dress.

"Chauncey is having a party tonight."

"Go."

"I will," Joey said hesitantly, "I was hoping you would go with me."

Without looking at Joey, I said, "If we are going to say goodbye Joey, have it be now."

"Marion, don't be like this. Please. I hate that this is the way things are. Let's just go to Chauncey's and have a fun night."

"Joey, do you really know me?"

"Yes. You are going to say no."

"How can you expect me to go to Chauncey's and pretend I am having a good time as everyone gets drunk on wine coolers?"

"I don't. But, Marion, please, I don't want to end like this. I think I love you."

"Well, good thing you're leaving before you figured that out."

Joey turned me around. At that time, I only managed to put my panties on. Joey holding my naked torso in his arms made me too vulnerable than I preferred. Still, I felt safer than I would in the future.

"Look, I don't want to leave you. After all these years of thinking you only thought of me like a brother, to have you be my girl….this is the worst time. I get it. But Marion, I have nothing here."

"I'm not enough?"

"You're more than enough. But let's get real. How long can I be holed up in your room before Daddy Portwood figures out I'm here?"

"It doesn't matter."

"I'm eighteen, Marion. He can have me arrested me for raping you just because you are seventeen. When do you turn eighteen anyways?"

"In March."

"It's May. I turn nineteen in July. It's too big of an age gap for any judge."

"The age of consent here is sixteen. Whatever, Joey. Go to California if you are so hell-bent on going. There are plenty of girls down there."

"But the Northern girl with the way she kisses, she gets her boyfriend warm at night. I wish she could be a California girl."

Joey started to kiss me. I pushed him away and sat on my bed.

"I am a British Invasion fan. I never cared for the Beach Boys that much."

Joey crawled to me and laid me down. Kissing my neck, he sang, "Love, Love me Do. You Know I love you. I'll always be…"

Before he could finish Lennon's and McCartney's lyrics, I put my finger to his lips.

"Don't make promises you can't keep."

"I'll promise you this; I'll be at the fort at five pm tomorrow. Meet me there."

"I'll try."

Joey laid down on my chest.

"Don't you have to go to Chauncey's?" I asked.

"Not until tonight. I am sleeping right here until it is time to leave."

Joey kept that promise. Once I heard his even breath, I wrapped us in a blanket. He slept a long while. When he woke up, he begged me to make love. Afterward, he begged me to go to Chauncey's house. I didn't give into that. I wrapped myself in my blanket and led him to the door.

"See you tomorrow," I said as I closed the door with a kiss.

I quickly got dressed and went downstairs. My parents kept an office area in the downstairs common area of our spilt-level. All shared financial documents were stored there. It was the only office kept until Mom realized a second child wasn't coming. She made the second bedroom her "spiritual study" where my father was forbidden to enter.

I appoarched the six-foot file cabinet. I opened the drawers going through old tax returns and pay stubs. Finally, I found a folder labeled, "Marion's saving bonds."

My Grandmother Portwood didn't believe in Christmas and Birthday presents. For those holidays she gave me five hundred dollars in saving bonds with the intent to have it pay for my college. By the time she died, I have accumulated ten thousand dollars in bonds. I grabbed them, ran upstairs, and stashed them in my bookbag. I spent the rest of the night pretending to do my homework. I would look up the answers in the back of my textbook then added stochastic equations to make it look like I did the work.

My parents came home early evening. Mother kissed me on the forehead.

"You are looking better, Honey. You just needed a chance to rest."

"I did. How was the pow-pow?"

"It would have been fun if it wasn't…"

Dad shook his head and cleared his throat. "At least you got your homework figured out."

"Somewhat."

"We'll work more on it tomorrow."

My parents went their separate ways. I went to bed.

Whenever my parents spent time with my Native American relatives, Dad would say something my mother would take for rudeness. They never talked the next day. My father went out at three. Mom spent the entire day in her study. Luckily, I was left to my own device at five.

I went to the fort with the bonds in my sweatshirt pocket. Joey met me with a smile. He lifted a bag.

"Hey! I got us Buca!"

"How did you get to Saint Paul?" I asked.

"I borrowed a car from my friend. He is going to let me take it to the Grey Hound Station tomorrow and leave it there for me to pick up. I asked if I could have it tonight to give you a proper date. So I picked you up some fine Italian food. It's not as good as Mom makes it, but it is not bad. I also scored some wine!"

Joey took out the spaghetti, chicken parmigiana, and cannoli out of the bag. He patted a spot on the sheet next to him. Then Joey pulled out a peach wine cooler from his backpack. I sat down, but I didn't take the wine cooler he offered.

"How was Chauncey's?"

"A little lame, but it was the last time I'd see everyone. I may go in for first period to say goodbye. Eat!"

"How'd you get the money for all this?"

Joey stuck a cannoli in my mouth. "This is our last night, Marion. I didn't expect to get interrogated. If you must know, I stuck into my mom's apartment knowing she would be at church. I stole whatever cash my stepfather had laying around. I'm not proud of it so let's end this conversation."

I bit into the cannoli and place the rest down on the plate Joey provided. I pulled out the saving bonds.

"Here is ten thousand dollars."

"I'm not taking your money, Marion."

"That's right. I will share it with you on our journey."

"Come again?"

"I am going with you."

Joey sighed. "Marion, I'd love it if you will, but it's not safe for you. I might be sleeping in bathrooms at rest stops."

"You won't if we have my money. I already thought it through. We will cash one in a new city. It will throw off their scent when they search for us."

"Whose they? Your parents?"

I crossed my arms over my chest. "The choice is yours, Joey. I leave with you and we have ten thousand dollars. Or you can leave alone knowing I will hate you forever."

Joey put down his plate. "Damn it, Marion…"

"You make your choice now."

"Well, having you around is the more appealing choice. Fine. You're coming. "

I smiled, "I can sneak you into my house after we finish dinner and mess around here for old time sake. Then we can sneak out after first period."

Joey smirked. "You are so romantic bossing me around like that."

He didn't mind following my directions. That was our last night together in our beloved sanctuary.

7

It's been two weeks since the accident. All I have accomplished is sitting around the house, watching the entire series of "Downton Abbey." Irving gets to work later than usual. He intends to take care of me. I find it irritating. I accepted the state of our marriage long ago. I don't want to give into a change that would eventually revert to the status quo.

I emerge from my bedroom to find Irving has made the coffee. He's already poured me a cup. Like a dutiful wife, I walk to the table as he motions to my chair. I sit and take a sip. I wish Irving will read whatever article he has on his smartphone or go to his study. Instead, he sits across from me aware of the awkwardness in between us.

"I was thinking," Irving says as I sip my coffee, "the Prior Lake Players are doing a production of 'Who's Afraid of Virginia Wolf?' tomorrow night. I thought we should go."

I put down my cup. I wait for a playful smirk to arise on Irving's face, but I do not see any.

"You are joking right?"

"Well, Marion, who is afraid of Virginia Wolf?"

"You are for one. So am I. Our hatred of her work is the foundation of our relationship."

"Well, my dear, the play isn't even about Virginia Woolf."

"I know very well what it is about!" I shout, "It is about an infertile couple who have nothing better to do than to harass younger couples! You sincerely don't expect I would take an interest in the story after losing my own baby now!"

"I just thought it would be a bit of fun," Irving replies baffled, "we haven't attended a play in ages. I thought you would enjoy the change of pace."

Irving gives me a scolding look that my behavior is hostile. I breathe a sigh in attempts to center myself.

"No offense to the Prior Lake Players, I am sure they are excellent. I just don't see the point in driving the hour to Prior Lake when we have a community theater five minutes from our house. The Bloomington Art Center is putting on 'The Best Little Whore House in Texas.' The Guthrie and the Ordway are only twenty-five minutes away, and they are world renowned."

Irving's face begins to flush. "I thought about going somewhere new for a change."

"I believe that the only reason for your horrid suggestion is that someone you fancy is playing the role of Honey. You wish to support her, but you feel obligated to play the doting husband giving my condition."

Irving becomes stonefaced. I am not assuaged.

"Your silence speaks volumes. That is quite alright. I release you from your duties tomorrow evening."

"Marion," Irving pleads as I arise from my chair. I quickly retreat to my room with my coffee. Sitting on my desk, I log into my email. There I see a reminder that I have a session with Dr. Kroll. I hear my father's footsteps coming up the stairs then greets Irving.

"How is Marion?" he asks.

"She's changed since the accident," Irving replies.

"That is to be expected," I heard Father says.

"These past four months, Mitchell, she has walked with a sense of purpose. She was radiant and vivacious. She has since reverted to her complaisant ways now that she lost the baby."

"Complaisant is good," Father replies, "That is the way she ought to be."

"Are you sure?

"When she was of strong will, she put me through hell. I don't mean to sound misogynistic, but complicity in a woman is a desirable trait. If her mother were more agreeable to my will, I'd still be married. My biggest fear for the two of you was that the baby would allow her to form her own ideas. We can't have that now, can we?"

"She still vehemently hates Virginia Woolf," Irving replies in passing.

I hear shuffling until the garage door closes. Compliancy? For real? No wonder why my mother left. All the pot in the world couldn't assuage the neglect in her marriage. I just wish she'd taken me with her.

Given that I have an appointment with Dr. Kroll, I need a quick shower then I am off to Fairview Hospital. Dr. Kroll's practice is in an adjoining building. I make sure to arrive on time. From experience, psychologists mark a demerit in your file if you are late. One must be a saint to shake off a diagnosis of mental illness.

Dr. Kroll comes into the waiting room wearing an uptight cardigan. This time it is a brick color.

"Ms. Palavar, you may come into my office."

I follow Dr. Kroll three steps behind to his office. I enter what is likely an old hospital room made into a Freudian dream. Dr. Kroll has a mahogany bookcase filled with leather bound books. On top of it is a globe. With a vinyl armchair and matching couch, I'd assume it was an academic office. Dr.Kroll motions me to the couch. I sit down. He sits on the arm chair.

"How is the day, Marion?"

"Good," I reply.

"Reason?"

I am surprised at Dr. Kroll's blunt manner. I have been in these halls enough time that a professional should build a rapport with their victim…I mean client before getting into the reasons why they are here.

"It is simply the feedback I received this morning," I answered.

"Describe."

"Irving, my husband, told my father that I've become complaisant and my father advised that is good."

Dr. Kroll stops writing in his folder. "Do you don't find that strange?"

"Should I?"

"I would find it disturbing if you didn't."

"Are you Irish?"

Dr. Kroll arched his eyebrow. "I don't see what my nationality has to do with anything."

"I just noticed your dark hair and pale skin. The combination is not a typical Anglo trait."

"I do not wish to disclose my nationality," Dr. Kroll advised.

"It's not that I wish to be weird or anything," I explained, "it is just that a psychologist must practice cultural competency. I have an Anglo father and husband alike. It is the expectation that I am to comply as an Anglo woman."

Dr. Kroll taps on his clipboard. I am worried. I told the male doctor what he should want to hear. By the avoidance of looking into my eyes and the awkward pause after my explanation, it is evident I have done the opposite.

"Marion, why do you assume you're knowledgeable in therapeutic competencies?"

"Therapy's been a revolving door in my life for the last twenty-some years."

"Fair enough. You talk about the Anglo culture. Have you ever had interacted with anyone outside of your ethnicity?"

"My mother's family had Dakota blood."

"And romantic relations?"

"My first boyfriend was Italian American. Sicilian I think."

"Did he expect you to be complaisant?"

"No. Joey didn't expect anything from me," I murmured. "To him, I was enough. I didn't have to change at all."

"Enough?"

"The myth all women try to achieve," I explained. "All a woman wants to be is enough for their partner."

Dr. Kroll arched his eyebrow at me again.

"I understand that the standard is unattainable. Men have various needs that cannot be satisfied within the realm of monogamy. Besides, Joey died when we were so young. If he lived, he would have dumped me for a woman in closer proximity. Or maybe we would have preferred a woman skilled at oral sex and didn't need to read a woman's magazine to learn how to initiate relations. Either way, had Joey lived, I would have been met with the reality that I wasn't enough."

"The concept of enough," repeats Dr. Kroll. "It is just a myth to you?"

"It is an unattainable goal, yes."

Dr. Kroll closes his folder. "We have covered enough."

"Dr. Kroll, I've only sat with you for twenty minutes."

"Enough can be attainable," Dr. Kroll says flippantly. "Why don't you go home and ponder that?"

"Very well," I say.

I get up and walk to the door. Given my suicidal history, I fear my father would still have rights to my medical records. Did he release all rights to Irving?

"You will mark that I am complaisant?"

"I will mark want is in your best interest. Maybe you need to go home and think of what that may be," Dr. Kroll says sternly.

I leave and go to the Southdale mall across the street. At least I could get a pretzel there. Dr. Kroll is such a funny doctor. I just told him I was aware of my best interest. I confessed Joey's death causes me to idolize him. Frankly, I don't understand why he doesn't accept my mindfulness. I told him what he wanted to hear. I am an excellent Anglo.

As I munch on my cinnamon sugar pretzel on the escalator, I realize my faux pas. Why did I refer sexual relations with Joey to Dr. Kroll? Promiscuity is not an indicator of one being mentally sound. Despite spans of celibacy during my marriage, the fact I acted on my teenage attraction will forever label me a whore. Now I have cursed myself years of interrogation with the stoic Dr. Kroll. Why did I do that?

I wander down the halls. I see teenagers holding hands. I see women my age carry themselves with the confidence I don't possess. I wonder how these young people love openly. I wish I knew how these women walk as if life's perils can't touch them. I walk out of the mall with one wish for myself: If only...

8

"You've been quiet all weekend," Father said as he drove me to school.

"I've just been busy figuring things out," I said.

"Any thoughts?"

"Still figuring," I replied.

"I found out Augsburg College has a post-secondary program for seniors," Father said. "It isn't a prestigious as Saint Catherine's, but it will let you possibly attend full-time next year."

I replied with a small grunt. Father shuffled me out of the house this morning. Mom was still home because her meetings at the Native American Resource Center were later in the morning. I want to say more to her than a simple goodbye. Then again, if I had stayed, there would be a chance I'd say some sappy parting words and give myself away. I guessed getting pushed out the door was a good thing.

Dad pulled up to school. I turned to him than froze. Questions flooded my mind at the worst possible moment. Things about our lives came up in past arguments between my parents throughout the years. My parents got married during a whirlwind summer at a spiritual retreat. They were on the brink of separation when my mother discovered she was pregnant. My father has stated that the reason he stayed was to prevent me from being raised on the reservation. I wanted to ask him why he stayed when he resented my mother and me. I wanted to know if he really thought I could reach wherever he thought I could reach. He was the man I never wanted to see again: the man who loathed my existence but couldn't leave me alone. I realized I truly didn't have anything to say to him. I could deceive him with a clear conscious.

"Have a good day, Dad."

I didn't wait for a reply when I got out of the car. I shut the door and walked as if this was a regular day of school. Other students crowded around the front steps to the school. The bell rang. Everyone dispersed. Standing at the front door was Joey.

He walked out and embraced me.

"How did you get out of the house?"

"I escaped when you went to the shower."

"How?"

"Your mother was on the phone and your father was downstairs. I made a quick run to the park where I stashed the car. Either way, we have to leave now if we are going to cash one of those bonds and make the bus. You packed your backpack with what you need?"

I lifted my blue Jansport backpack. "I certainly didn't pack it with books."

"Good," he said, "let's get going."

I hopped into a white sedan, and we left the school behind.

"I know of a place in Saint Paul where they cash any check no questions asked," Joey said.

"How do you know of a place?" I asked.

"The ass hat my mom is married to has a gambling problem," Joey said as he ushered me to the car. "Look, if we are going to do this, you are going to have to trust me, got it? If you don't trust me, let me know right now and we can forget that I allowed you to come along. I am risking my ass aiding in your runaway scheme."

I opened the car door.

"Trust goes both ways, Joey."

Joey followed me into the car.

"Fine. Just trust me on this one."

Joey drove me into Saint Paul on the north side of University Street. Hmong and African American people walked the street. I pulled out two of my bonds. Joey got out and opened the door for me. He looked nervous walking the parking lot of The Cash 'N Check.

"Are you okay?"

"I don't mean to sound racist, but I do not like the fact that we are the only white people in the area. Do you?"

"I'm often the only white person visiting the relatives on the reservation," I replied. "I am used to being the lone white girl. Don't worry. We are more likely to be raped and murdered by white men."

I linked my arm around Joey. Joey stood up straighter, puffing his chest out slightly. He reminded me of a wounded parrot pretending to be tough, so he didn't become pray. Quickly, we walked into Cash 'n Check signed the bonds and walked out with a thousand dollars. Joey ushered me out to the car as fast as he could without being conspicuous. As soon as we were in the car, Joey locked the doors and sped off.

The bus depot was only a couple of blocks. I went into the bathroom as he purchased tickets. There I changed my shirt into a black hoodie I long forgotten about until I searched for clothes for Joey that Friday. I figured if I forgot I had it, so would my parents. I took my travel size tube of hair gel and began to spike my hair. I wasn't unrecognizable, but no one could identify me at a quick glance.

Joey sat on a bench as I emerged from the bathroom. I sat next to him. He looked down at the ground. I knew he was scared. I wanted to comfort him, but I was afraid that if I showed him any affections, it would give ourselves away. If the school called truancy, my parents might be looking for me. I'm just glad I had wiped my browser history before I left.

"You look like a punk," Joey commented without looking up from the ground.

"Thanks," I replied dryly. "Do you have our tickets?"

Joey handed me my bus ticket.

"Saint Louis?"

"If we pay for the entire way to California, anyone looking for us will know our destination. I figure, we'll buy tickets at each stop and check in with my cousin. If he tells me there is heat on our location, we'll change our plans."

"To what?"

"I don't know, Marion! Trust me to think of something! Even digging a hole to hide in until you are eighteen is better than turning back."

Joey looked over at the departure screen, and then he casually wrapped his arm around me. I felt a vibration underneath his sweatshirt.

"Bus 24 is boarding. That's our bus let's go."

Joey walked me to the bus. On the way, he stopped at the trash can. He unclipped his pager from his jean and tossed it into the trash.

We walked onto the bus and moved to the available seat closet to the back. Once we found seats, we stashed our backpacks underneath. I sat on the window seat. I leaned against a tensed Joey. After an eternity, the bus doors closed. Finally, the bus pulled out of the terminal.

When the bus entered Interstate 35, Joey let a sigh of relief. "We made it."

"I'll feel better when we are out of Minnesota.'

Joey leaned back and wrapped his arm around me. I watch the city view become rural. When I saw the signs for the Iowa state line, I asked, "Why did you throw your pager away?"

"I have no need for it now," Joey answered. "My mother has been paging me. She threw me out of the house. She doesn't deserve to know where I am."

"Are you going to miss this place?"

My head bounced on Joey's chest as he shrugged.

"It wasn't all bad. I made friends here. I don't know. If I wasn't leaving with you, I might miss it more than I do. How about you?"

"I was born here, but I never fit in here."

"You fit in with me."

"Only in the woods."

Joey responded with a grunt. I stared at the window. We sat in silent bliss as the cornfields of Iowa came into view.

"Joey, if you loved me all those years, how come you never said anything?"

"Umm," Joey said, "I didn't want to risk losing our friendship if you didn't feel the same."

"That's the dumbest answer."

"What do you want me to say? That I can't resist pretty things who throw themselves at me?"

"That would be the truth."

"I'm pretty. I threw myself at you. You took the bait," Joey bent over and kissed my head. "Boys and girls aren't different."

"I am," I replied, "You got into my pants because I love you."

"I love you too," Joey whispered into my hair. "If this thing is going to work, you have to trust that I do."

"I will."

We made out during the ride through Iowa. If only I could relive our passionate times. As Joey's death inched into the two digit mark, I started to question that he loved me. Soon, after I lost the baby, I received a strange call reminding me I should have trusted him all along.

9

It is now two weeks after I returned from the hospital. I have another two weeks of leave; yet, I have regained my mobility. With the help of the Vicodin, I can function with minimal pain. Binge watching shows on all of our streaming services was fun for the first week. The only human contact I had is Irving with an occasional visit from my father. I have seen Doctor Kroll twice now. I am not sure if he counts as human. I view him as a random question generator. The last visit, he asked general questions regarding my nationalities to decipher what parts of me were Anglo. I found the session an unnecessary way to spend an hour.

Irving is dressed in his usual button-down shirt and sweater. He wears solid colors but doesn't care if the color of his shirt and sweater clashes. Today's choice is a neon orange shirt pair with a hunter green sweater. I can tell it is November now. He is growing a beard, although he claims it is for winter instead of "Movember," whatever that is. He looks at me in disbelief as I come out of my bedroom in wearing my black vintage sweater set with a skirt.

"Why are we dressed up today?"

"I'm returning to work."

"Why?"

"Because it is time."

"If you can be finished getting ready in fifteen minutes, please do so. I have to be in my office early today because it is the editing workshops for my Freshman Comp students this week."

"You don't need to wait for me. I can drive myself."

"You are on Vicodin," Irving reminds me. "You shouldn't be driving. In fact, you shouldn't be trying to do your job while on heavy medication. Remember what happened to Jessica Hank after she returned from her appendectomy?"

Jessica Hank is my co-worker in the administration office at Nicollet. Last spring for fall registration, she mixed up half the students' enrollment, causing a huge mess the first week of fall semester. She happened to be on her honeymoon the following week, leaving me to do her rework.

"Nothing happened to her," I say, "She kept her job. You defended her."

"Well, now is time for spring registration. Let's avoid the hassle this time. Stay home."

"Fine!" I screamed.

Irving steps back against the counter. He gives me the self-righteous startled look indicating I've demonstrated too much emotion for his liking.

"Have it your way! I am a grown woman who can make her own decisions. But, if you think you can make better decisions for me, so be it. I am no mood to argue with you or to have you talk to me as if I am a little child to preserve your lunch plans with Jessica Hank."

Irving nods then talks in his lecturing tone, "Very well. Yes, I did intend to have lunch with Jessica today. It isn't odd for men to be friends with other women in the workplace."

"It is rather odd for a married woman to refer a co-worker's husband as her 'work husband'. If it is not strange, it is entirely disrespectful."

"I wasn't aware you cared."

"Fortunately for you, caring is not a founding value in our relationship."

I retreat to my room. Irving walks over and knocks. I don't answer. He doesn't come in. It is our unspoken rule. Unspoken rules are the cornerstone of our marriage. One is that I do not inquire who he sees socially. The second is that he is not to hover over my day to day operations (as long as I am in line with my father's unspoken rules). The pregnancy forced us to reexamine our ways. We started talking. We were on our way to forming a partnership. The baby is gone. Irving is back to being an extension of my father. I don't know if I love Irving enough to fight and preserve our change.

I change into jeans and a Nicollet sweatshirt. Contrary to my father's opinion, Nicollet is an excellent college. I am proud to be its alumnus and employee.

I make myself a cup of coffee. Randomly surfing on my smartphone, I end up on my weather app. I see that it is unseasonably warm and take my coffee to the deck. I stand out there looking out into the woods.

For the last twenty years, I lived to survive. My father didn't exactly arrange Irving and me; still, our marriage was his wish. I like Irving enough to live with him as long as it removes me from my father's conservatorium. Now, with the baby come and gone through my womb, I am questioning the life I allowed. If there is more of it for me, now can't be the time to change it. Not with my mental health being under the microscope this moment.

I hear the faint sound of the phone ringing from the inside. I enter, and our one landline phone is beeping. We kept the landline number when our internet company sold us on one of those bundling packages. No one calls us on the number.

"Hello?" I answer.

"Hello, does a Marion Portwood reside at this number?" a man with a coastal accent asks.

"May I ask who is calling?"

"Are you Marion Portwood?"

"May I ask your business?" I say annoyed.

"My name is Marty Dean. You were dating my cousin, Joey Troli."

I nearly drop the phone. Joey? What would business relating to Joey have anything to do with me?

"Ms. Portwood? Ms. Portwood, are you there?"

I pick up the phone. "Yes, I am here."

"Good! I wasn't sure if I had the right number. Joey had it in his pocket twenty years ago. Numbers changes. No one has a landline anymore."

"You are calling me about Joey?"

"I'm calling you to tell you your house is ready."

10

We pulled into Saint Louis late into the night. Joey grabbed my hand as we walked off the bus. We walked straight to a pay phone.

"What should I dial?" he asked, "1-800-COLLECT or C-A-L-L-A-T-T?"

"Depends on which David is your favorite."

"Like Arquette better than Spade," he answered.

Joey dialed collect and stated his name. I leaned against the booth with my eyes closed as Joey spoke.

"Hey, Marty. It's Joe...What?"

I opened my eyes.

"Man, I figured it would happen. Just not so soon...Alright...It'd be another ten months, Man...Tell, Aunt Teressa not to worry. I'll figure something out."

After a few "uh-huh's," Joey hung up.

"My cousin came home to a message from the Bloomington Police Department on the machine."

"How did they know where we were going?" I asked.

Joey checked his watch. "It's ten o'clock now, which means schools been out for eight hours. Your parents figured out you never came home and called the police. The police either talked to my mom..."

"Or looked at recent calls from the cordless phone and got your cousin's number," I added.

"Forgot about that!"

I leaned back against the booth. "What are we going to do? We don't know how hot the cops are on our tail."

"It's the Bloomington police," Joey replied. "They only have jurisdiction in Bloomington, Minnesota. They aren't going to send the FBI after you, Marion, if that is what you are worried about. We aien't going back to Minnesota. However, if they called my aunt's house, they have informed the Anaheim Police that a runaway is coming to town. California is out of the question now."

We only used one hundred dollars from my first bond check. Given that we traveled by bus, we could afford a variety of locations. I looked at the bulletin listing departures. I must have scanned it five times before realizing that my eyes always lingered on Arizona.

"Where is the Grand Canyon location?" I asked.

Joey rolled his eyes. "Arizona."

"I know Arizona! But where? Tucson? Phoenix? Prescott?"

"The Canyon is its own location," Joey answered. "I think Prescott is the closest of the cities you listed."

"Let's go there!"

"Why?"

"Think about it. The ride into Arizona is going to take all night. That will take care of tonight's shelter. The Southwest is warm. If any reason we have to sleep outside we won't catch hypothermia. There is a bevy of reservations in the area too. We could go to them when we need help."

"There are Dakota reservations in Arizona?"

"We can go to any reservation. All we need to do is claim that the white man is chasing us," I answered, "The people will let us in. You're tan enough to pass through the gate."

"Italians don't get confused with Native American," Joey remarked pointing to his face.

"Doesn't matter, I carry my tribal card," I replied. "Come on, let's get our tickets before the bus leaves. We can't be lingering here too long."

"You really want to go to Prescott?"

"That's the closest to the Canyon," I answered. "I've always wanted to see it. Eventually, we can inch our way towards it. Let's just get to Prescott and figure out things once we get there."

"Sounds good to me."

I handed Joey money for his ticket and pointed to the ticket counter at the far end. I went to the one in the middle. I figured if someone looking for the two of us, it was best not to buy the tickets together. The bus into Prescott left the bus terminal fifteen minutes after we loaded onto it. Joey led me to the back of the bus. The bench was the longest. We could both stretch out legs.

The sky was dark. We couldn't see anything. I leaned against the window. Joey leaned against the wall of the lavatory. He closed his eyes. I could see the pained look on his face, although he was hiding it.

"Once the heat dies down, we can head over to California," I said.

Joey opened his eyes. "It won't be safe to go there until you're eighteen. We got what? Ten more months to hide."

"I'm sorry."

"For what?"

"For being the reason you can't get to your family."

"It's better than leaving you behind and knowing you hate me for the rest of my life. With my dad dead and my mother abandoning me, I don't really have a family. I guess I'm an orphan now." Joey gave me a joking smile, "Are you going to take care of me?"

I leaned over and grabbed his hands. "Of course."

Joey wrapped me in his arms. We fell asleep in each other arms.

By sunrise, the bus pulled into the station at Downtown Prescott. Joey and I grabbed our bags and walked off the bus. Exiting the bus depot, we found ourselves among historical brick buildings. We walked the streets looking into boutiques and artisan cafes.

"This place remains me of Stillwater," I said, mentioning the tourist town on the Saint Croix River.

"I'm thinking of Saint Paul's Grand Avenue in the desert," Joey replied.

"You hung out in Saint Paul?"

"Only when my mother dragged me there," Joey answered. "She liked to buy her spices from a shop on the street."

We wander our way to a courtyard at the city hall. Joey put his backpack on the ground.

"We made it to Prescott. Now what?"

I scanned the area and pointed out West.

"That area seems to have some coffee houses. We could go to one and get a paper. Browse the want ads and housing listing."

"I don't think we can afford housing, Marion."

"We still have my bonds," I answered. "We could cash them for an apartment. Maybe we will find jobs. I am not afraid to work. Are you?"

"I'm not scared," Joey said. "I'm just realistic. I never had a job. I have no history. Do you have a job history?"

"Everyone starts somewhere," I commented. "We are going to start our work lives here."

We walked towards the avenue known as Whiskey Row. We found a place called "The Raven" that sold coffee. I got coffee and a scone. Joey got orange juice and an egg sandwich. We sat next to the window. Joey looked out onto Downtown Prescott. I bought a paper and scanned the want ads. As if it were meant to be, I found the perfect ad.

"Joey, I found the job that solves our problems."

Joey quit looking out the window. "What?"

"Prescott Inn is looking for maintenance men and house cleaners. They are willing to offer room and board with a small wage. Do you know how to fix anything?"

"My dad taught me how to fix cars. I haven't fixed one since he died."

"I can clean house," I said. "I helped my parents every Sunday. I'm going to call the number and see if we can get an interview."

"Be my guest," said Joey.

I went to a payphone and dialed the number from the ad. We were able to secure an interview within two hours. The barista told us the inn was only two blocks from The Raven. With her directions, we found we were able to find it.

The lobby of the Prescott Inn resembled an old fashion western brothel with its ornate woodwork. The top two floors could be seen from the balconies. I could imagine prostitutes leaning against them back in the day. Now it was quiet. I saw one man walk across the second-floor balcony. Other than him, the inn was a ghost town.

"May I help you?" a voice said from behind us.

We turned around to find a woman who resembled my mother. She had long blond hair and smooth tan skin.

"Yes, I am looking for Lily Thunderman."

"I'm her," said she quizzically.

I reached out my hand. "I'm Marion Portwood. You scheduled an interview with us."

"You are the girl I spoke with?"

"Yes."

Lily motion to a hallway. "Follow me."

Joey looked at me and shrugged. He didn't seem to have faith we would get the job. I kept a brave face. This interview may only be the one chance we would get. We just needed to convince Ms. Thunderman that we weren't some punk kids.

Lily led us into her office. She pulled up two chairs in front of her desk. We sat down. I looked around to see sculptures of medicine women and busts of warriors. She sat down with an uncertain smile.

"Are you Navajo?" I asked.

"I have Hopi blood, actually," Lily answered.

"I'm of Dakota blood!"

"Really? Your speech is rather English," Lily commented. "The Dakotas, uh. Aren't they based in the Northern Plains?"

"We're running from the white man," Joey said.

Heat rose from my face as Lily's eyebrows shot up.

"Running from the white man?"

"Yes, our mother is married to the white man," Joey explained. "He is cruel to us. He kicked us out despite the fact that our grade were good."

"That's all?"

"That all we can make sense of," I chuckled.

Lily tapped her pen against her desk.

"Here is what I am making sense of this meeting. The two of you are applying for the job because you need the room and board, not that you feel you meet the qualifications."

"She can clean, I can fix things," Joey said, "what other qualifications will you need?"

Lily sighed, "This isn't a no-tell motel. It is an inn. The families and couples that come to Downtown Prescott have high expectations of the quality of our service."

"We were set to some pretty high standards," Joey responded, "unfortunately by unreasonable people."

"Many of my patrons come off as unreasonable," Lily stated. "If the two of you are in trouble, I can recommend a couple of places the two of you can go to for help."

"We actually prefer to work and make our way," I responded. "Neither one of us wishes to be a charity case. Joey is right. We both were held to pretty high expectations. We both have strong work ethics. We just need someone to give us a chance."

Lily breathed another sigh. We sat in silence for a long while. Lily broke it with another awkward smile.

"Okay, if both of you are willing to work, I will give you a chance. If any of my patrons have a valid complaint, it may be grounds to terminate the both of you. Do you agree to my terms?"

"Yes, ma'am," we said.

"Okay," Lily said. "I only have one room available tonight for you to stay in."

"I'll sleep on the floor," Joey said.

"Okay, lucky for you the room has two beds," Lily said. "Why don't I show you to your room and you can fill out these payroll papers. I will need copies of your identifications."

Joey pulled out his wallet and handed her his social security card. I pulled out my tribal card. Lily put them on her desk and motioned us to follow her. We walked to a corner room on the first floor.

The room was a standard hotel room. It had two full bed, a dresser with a television sitting on it, and an adjoining bathroom.

"I know it is not much, but it will have to do," Lily said. "Please fill out the form right away. I will back here shortly with your uniforms. I require you to wear them while you are working."

"Thank you," I said.

Lily nodded and left. Joey and I filled out our forms. We had completed them before Lily returned with Joey's coveralls, my duster, and two peanut butter sandwiches.

"I'll see you at six a.m. in my office tomorrow morning," she said,"That is when the work day begins. Don't be late."

"Thank you," I said.

"Thanks," Joey said.

The moment Lily closed the doors, Joey jumped me onto a bed. He started kissing me.

"You know, I am not going to sleep in other bed."

"Good thing you don't snore."

"May I?"

"May you what?"

With a kiss after each word, Joey asked, "May? I? Do? You?"

"Joey, we ran away together. You don't have to ask for anymore. My consent is implied until further notice."

Joey laughed. "Let's just keep the noise down. As long as Lily thinks we are related, she'll let us share the same room."

I put my finger up to my lip. Joey kissed it away. We made love in celebration of our new freedom.

During the best two weeks of my life I worked harder than I ever had. We woke up at five in the morning to report for work at six. For ten hours, I scrubbed the twenty rooms of the Prescott Inn as Joey made repairs inside and outside. Once we finished our work, Joey and I took our bath, then soaked our uniforms and underwear in the tub. The dry Arizona heat dried our clothes by the next morning. We spent the night eating peanut butter sandwiches and making love. Difficult to believe, the best time of my life could be summed up in a paragraph.

One day, I found a woman's magazine in the trash while cleaning a room after check out. I brought it back and shown Joey the articles giving sexual advice. Joey flipped through the magazine.

"Guys don't like that. They don't like that. You really want to try that?"

I nodded.

"Okay. We are trying that."

On the second Friday, Lily called us into her office. We walked in with apprehension.

"The both of you are doing good work," she said. "Here is your first paycheck. Don't spend it all in one place."

We opened the envelopes.

"What are we going to do with them?" I asked.

Lily's eyebrows shot up. "You should put them in the bank."

"Right," Joey said, "Thank you! We promise not to spend it all in one place.

We left Lily's office and headed to the room. Habitually I took off my clothes. As I was about to become completely nude, Joey said, "Keep your underwear on. We are going out."

"Out? Where?"

"We got money. The drug store cashes checks. We can stop there, cash checks, and buy you some new underwear. Maybe we can have a real date. The Raven serves food."

"I need a bath first," I said. "Besides, I packed a couple of extra pairs of underwear for our journey."

Joey walked up to me. "Okay, our bath first."

He kissed me then pulled down my underwear.

An hour later, we were bathed, laid, and our laundry hung. Joey and I walked out in our jeans for the first time in two weeks. He wore his Clash T-shirt. I wore my black tank top. We walked the streets of Downtown Prescott cashing our checks and looking into shop windows. I bought a bar of agave goat milk soap at a hippie boutique. The soap the inn provided dried out my skin.

We made it to The Raven. We ordered iced green tea and fancy burgers. A band was setting up to play. Joey and I sat at the window again.

"This will be the first time I heard live music that's not classical," I said.

"You've never been to a concert?"

"Only at Orchestra Hall," I said. "You?"

"An old girlfriend dragged me to see Alanis Morrisette."

"Dragged you! I would have loved to have seen her."

"If we can get to any venue for her tour with Tori Amos, I'll take you."

I grabbed his hands across the table and giggled. "You are only saying that because we can't afford it."

Joey shrugged. "We barely spent money these past two weeks. We could save up and head out to Phoenix."

"But we work seven days a week," I pointed out.

"Lily has other employees. She can give us the day off."

I lean back in my chair. The band started the sound check. Our food came, and we began to eat. I looked out at the artisan town in the desert as the sun shone on City Hall. Everything looked vibrant.

"I don't want to live at the inn forever, but I would like to stay in Prescott," I said. "I could get my GED, and we can attend the community college here. I just love the place. Being here makes me feel so alive!"

Joey gave a slight smile. "We can start planning in ten months. Right now, let's keep laying low."

"Joey, this is the first time I can plan my own life."

Joey kissed my hand. "When you turn eighteen, those plans will become a reality."

"Really? Will you stay here with me?"

"I would like to get out to California. Who knows, maybe by the time we get out there, it will only be for a visit. Heck, once you turn eighteen, we could use the rest of the bonds to buy a mobile home. We can just go anywhere we want, and we'd be home."

I lifted my glass. "To the rest of our lives."

Joey clinked his glass to mine. "I promise you. I am going to buy you a home. The moment you are eighteen, I'll get you a home."

"Us a home," I corrected.

I spent the night basking in excitement and hope. When we toasted, we didn't know Joey's life ended in a week. I didn't feel excitement again until I found out I was pregnant. That ended.

Now, I walk into the woods with apprehension. Is it trouble or excitement around the corner?

11

I walk out the garage and around the fence. The trees grew during the last twenty-one years. Thankfully, there is still a clearing into the park. I walk through the trees. I am surprised to see a trash can on the path. I turn right and proceed in a direction I never forgot.

This is really insane. Miles Creek is a park reservation. The city of Bloomington forbids construction on the land. Yet, as I wander on the path, I see that the park's borders have shrunk, given way to modern looking houses.

I pass by the sewer and the dam. Both now sport decorative railings. By instinct, I continue under the highway bridge and walk a couple of turns until I am at the bottom of a tree-covered hill. As I walk, I know that I am running a fool's errand. There is no house. If there is a cousin of Joey's in Bloomington, he's most likely to kill me to avenge Joey's death. Still, I walk. Certain death is better than living in the limbo I currently reside.

A man stands at the end of the hill. He has Joey's dark hair, but it is thining. He wears an open black leather jacket. He has no hat or gloves. I find that funny because I remember Joey mentioning that Marty lived in California. He sees me, and within seconds I am engulfed into an embrace.

"Marion! How you doing? Gosh, you look the same. What has it been? Twenty years since Joey died and you still look the same. Accept your hair is longer."

We break the embrace. I find my fingers exploring the ends of my bob haircut resting against my chin. I grew my hair out for my wedding. I found long hair tenuous to manage. Instead of going back to my pixie cut, I kept my femininity with a bob.

"Well, it's all up there," he says, pointing to the hill. "Let me show you around."

We climb the hill to a thick cluster of five-year-old maple trees. Marty opens a hidden door made of tree bark. On the other side is a living room.

"Here we are," Marty says.

We walk into a one-room house in trees. The furniture is rustics. I can tell its structure consists of repurposed materials. There is a small sink next to a tiny wood burning stove. To the side is a loft over a coat closet. Above us was nothing but sky and tree leaves.

"Isn't this great?" Marty exclaimed, "It's a little earth ship."

"An earth ship?"

Marty walked around pointing out features as he explained them.

"All of this is made from recycled materials for sustainable living. The wall is made from construction scraps over recycled tires for insulation. The sink works because we had leftover pipes from a project. The water source is the creek. You may want to buy some iodine tablets to sterilize your drinking water. The loft could fit a twin mattress, or you can sleep on the futon. You can burn wood to light the stove, but I added it for aesthetics. I made the ceiling a skylight to provide natural heat. Around the skylight are solar panels that will store energy for the night. There are only two outlets in here. The one thing I couldn't do is I install a toilet or shower. I nearly got caught laying down the pipes for the sink. I figured that this was a hideout, not a residence."

I walk the room in awe. This would be the hideout Joey and I would build if he were alive now. I touch the furniture with the handmade cushions. I open the door and walk out. Turning, I see the trees surrounding the dwelling. From five feet away, I can't tell a tiny house stands in the middle. Marty stands at the doorway.

"Did you plant the trees yourself?"

"Yes. Joey wanted the house to be like the fort you guys made. Once I had the walls up, I planted the maple trees. Now, come here. I have another thing to show you."

I walk into the house. Marty closes the door. He opens a look out window.

" You don't have to open the door to see who is around."

Marty closes the peephole in the door. I walk around the house carefully looking at the rustic furniture. There was a wooden table made of recycled wooden posts. It appeared from a stairwell. The table had two chairs. The futon is made with decorative metal fencing painted white. Next to it was white painted wood table. Sitting on top of the table is a lovely pewter frame of twisted roses. Inside is a picture I only got to see in my mind's eye these last twenty years: Joey and me in our prom attire.

"Sorry the background is blurry," Marty comments, "I fished it out of Joey's mom's trash can after the funeral. She burned a cigarette hole in the corner. I scanned it and blurred the background with my photo editor."

"She didn't think too kindly of me when Joey died."

"She shouldn't have been hateful towards you. You had nothing to do with his death.

I look at Marty. "How? Why? Why did you do all of this?"

Marty opens the door.

"It is what Joey wanted," he says. "I'll leave you be to take this all in."

He ducks out before I can open my mouth to tell him to stay. I sit down and stare at the photo. I hate to admit I started to forget what his face looked like exactly. I was shunned at his funeral. I clutch the picture to my heart as memories of that horrible time flood into my mind.

12

The last day I saw Joey alive began as normal. We woke, dressed in our uniforms, had toast and went to work. Such a cliché thing to say, I know. All days have standard beginnings, even the most tragic.

There is one moment about the day I am thankful for. Joey was fixing the bathroom fan in a room I had to clean. He stood on the counter as he unscrewed the cover. The temperature rose to eighty that week. Joey rolled the sleeves of his coveralls over his shoulders. I stood watching his muscular arms screw in the vent. After he had tightened the last screw, he looked down at me.

"What's up?"

"Nothing," I said, "Just checking out your biceps."

Joey looked down at me and smiled." I am done with my morning job list."

He jumped down from the counter. We started to kiss. Joey lifted me onto the counter. He began unbuttoning my uniform.

"What are you doing?"

" I think it's obvious," Joey replied.

"We can't do that here. Lily will have our hides if she catches us in here."

Joey took me by the hand. We walked into our room. Within seconds he unzipped his coveralls and had me down on the bed with my skirt hiked up and my panties off. Our lovemaking was brief. At the time I didn't mind. I was giddy over the bonus love making, believing it was in addition to our nightly ritual.

As I dressed, Joey rolled over to his side and closed his eyes.

"Are you seriously taking a nap right now?"

"My honey do list for the morning is completed. I am going to rest until lunch when Lily gives me another one."

I kissed him. "Lucky you."

I went back to the bathroom I abandoned moments ago. When I finished, I heard Lily's footsteps down the hall. I left the room to be met with her stern face.

"Marion, I need you to come with me to my office."

"Sure."

We walked to her office. I remember the feeling of dense ominous air as we had approached the door. I knew I was in trouble for something. Lily opened the door. It was my nightmare come true. Standing in the office was my father and two policemen.

"Marion Portwood?" one of the officers asked.

"It's her." My father answered gruffly.

Lily closed the door. I was trapped.

"Marion, where is Joey?"

By instinct, I lied. "Out."

"Where?" The other officer asked.

I shut up. I knew Lily wasn't going to allow me to return to work and Joey was in worst danger than me.

As if she could read my mind, Lily said, "It's no use trying to protect him. I intend to turn him over to the officers once he returns. I don't appreciate being conned by the two of you. I believed you were in genuine trouble. Instead, I unknowingly contributed to your delinquency. Now, I will be turning away people who actually need help because I can't trust anyone after this. You can be assured neither of you have a job here now."

The first officer said, "Mr. Portwood can take custody of his daughter. We need to find the boy."

"Marion, you need to tell the officer of Joey's whereabouts," Father ordered.

"Why? He didn't do anything."

"Your father told me that he forbade Joey to be your boyfriend," Lily commented. "I no longer have disillusioned he treated you sisterly."

"How we behave in private after work is nobody's business," I stated, "especially to the police."

The first officer looked at me, "Ms. Portwood, you are seventeen, correct?"

"Yes," Lily answered for me. "I have her identification and Mr. Troli's. Mr. Troli is eighteen."

Lily handed the cops the documentation. The second officer looked at the papers then to me.

"Ms. Portwood, the age of consent for Arizona is eighteen. Mr. Troli can be charged with statutory rape."

"I am pressing charges," Father declared.

The first officer, the bad cop, walked over to me. "You will tell us where Mr. Troli is now. Do you understand?"

"To the drug store," I lied, "we're out of condoms."

The two officers left. The first officer described Joey over the radio. I turn to leave.

"Excuse me, Marion," Lily protested, "I didn't permit you to leave."

"I am no longer your employee," I stated.

I ran to our room. It wasn't much of a headstart. My father and Lily were at the end of the hallway by the time I entered the room. Joey woke up when I slammed the door. He was about to curse until I put my finger to my lips. I quickly locked the door.

"What's going on?" he asked.

"My father is here. He brought the cops. The age of consent in Arizona is eighteen. You need to leave."

Joey cursed and put his on his clothes. The doorknob started to rattle. I could hear the click of the key. I pulled all of our money and the bonds then gave it to him. I backed myself into the door as Lily attempted to open the door.

"Do you mind?" I yelled. "I'm changing."

"Hurry up!" Father yelled.

Joey moved towards me. I pointed to the window. Joey kissed me.

"Stay away from the drug store," I whispered, "They are looking for you there."

Joey kissed my forehead then jumped out the window. There was nothing left to do but to change then face my fate.

As much as I hated when Father spoke, his silence was worst. That indicated something was brewing his head, often a punishment that I couldn't bear.

The flight back to Minnesota was two hours long. I leaned against the window and pretended to sleep. Tears continuously fell from my eyes. I thing I knew for sure is that I lost my freedom.

Mother was at the door when we entered the house. She embraced me.

"Patti," Father warned.

"She isn't getting away with anything, Mitch," Mother replied. "Go to your room, Marion."

Father excused himself to the downstairs office. Mother followed me to my room. I didn't have time to open the door.

"Do you know the hell you put us through?"

"Sorry," I grunted.

"Marion Shire, do not take that attitude with me. For two and a half weeks we thought the worst. You could be dead or in possession of an unsavory character forced to do unspeakable things."

"In truth, I was with Joey, safer traveling on a bus with him instead of staying in this house! Want to hear of a shocking thing we did? We got jobs! We found safe shelter! God forbid I live a life of my own."

"This isn't about you being prevented from living life, Marion! This is about you going behind our backs and leaving. You're only seventeen, Marion."

"Well, I survived."

Mother crossed her arms. "I talked to Joey's mom. She told me what happened with him and his stepdad. If you came to me, I could have helped him!"

"Like Dad would have let you!"

Mother sighed. She knew I was right. She also knew another uncomfortable fact.

"Well, I suppose living in this house is punishment enough," she said. "This is where you will remain until school starts next year. Now get to bed. The only place you'll be allowed to go the next couple of weeks is school."

Mother left and closed my door. I collapsed onto my bed. I wasn't going to be able to sleep.

The next day, I returned to school intending to resume my zombie walk. No such luck. Joey's friends met me at the front door.

"Hey, Portwood," Amber shouted, " Isn't Joey's cock is the best?"

I saluted Amber and proceeded to my first period to the fanfare of her cronies. Afterwards, I went to the library for second period. Erin looked up as I sat in the desk next to her.

"Hey," she whispered.

"Hi," I said.

"I heard you and Joey Troli tried eloping in Vegas."

"That didn't happen."

"I know," said Erin, "but it didn't stop the two of you from doing it."

"No, it did not," I replied nonchalantly.

Erin gasped. I pulled out my Trigonometry text book and attempted to tackle two months' worth of homework.

Finally, it was my lunch hour. Instead of buying lunch, I took my cash to the change machine. Every quarter went into the pay phone next to the vending machines. I pulled a piece of paper from my back pocket. Prior to leaving for school, I searched the call log on the cordless phone. I quickly dialed the number of Joey's aunt. It rang several times before I heard a familiar, "Hello?"

"Joey! You made it!"

"Marion?"

"Yes!"

Joey sighed on the other line. "Marion, you really shouldn't be calling."

"I just needed to know you were all right," I replied. "That you made it to California okay."

"I just got to my aunt, like hours ago. There were some times I saw cops and hid. It's been unreal. The cops called here again. Your father is going out of his way to see that I am locked up behind bars."

Attempting to twist the tight metal cord, I joked, "You did steal something valuable."

"Yeah, your virginity must be quite the prize."

"I meant my heart, you idiot."

"Look, Marion. I love you but I have to go."

A dial tone provided an abrupt soundtrack to the last time I heard Joey's voice. The only comfort I have is knowing he said he loved me when he ended our final conversation .

The next day, I went to school with a pocket full of quarters and excitement for talking to Joey again. My excitement forever vanished the moment I walked through the door.

One couldn't miss the monstrosity. In the middle of the hallway entrance stood a giant heart shaped collage made with pictures of Joey with every girlfriend he had in high school. That was, every girlfriend except me. I felt my heart chip as my eyes examined each picture. Once my eyes caught the inscription on the bottom, my heart shattered. In pink glitter script I read **Joey Troli 1980-1998**.

"His mother called Chauncey as soon as it happened," said Amber. I could see her talking to one of the other collage girls.

"Thank you for calling all of us," the other girl said. "I mean, we all loved Joey."

The corners of our eyes met. Amber reacted with, "Hey, true loves only! Back away!"

I complied because I knew if I stayed and fought with Amber, the bitch would have the satisfaction of seeing me cry. I turned and walked out the school. Once I was out, I ran to the creek. Once in the safety of our fort, I laid down and bawled. I didn't know the entire school day passed until my parents found me in the fort. Our walk home was the beginning of my dissent into the blur.

13

"What are you going to do today?" Irving asks the morning after.

I sit at the kitchen table, drinking coffee as Irving drinks his at the counter.

"Recover," I retort, "as I've been directed to do."

Looking towards Irving, I see him twist his face. It's his tell that he is unamused. He puts his cup in the sink. Mostly under his breath, he replies with, "Enjoy your day."

I hear the garage door close and proceed to get ready for the day. I hop into the shower for what I intend is the last time.

I sat for hours after Marty left contemplating how to utilize the treehouse. I'm sure Marty intended it to be a sanctuary for temporary escapement. Lacking a bathroom, the treehouse wasn't meant to be a tenement. I may have been out of touch with my Native American heritage the past two decades, but I do remember the skills I learned during the times I camped with mom's maternal side of the family. I know how to dig a toilet in the ground. I could fashion an outhouse out of twigs. Nicollet has showering facilities. Heck, on a rainy day, I can lather myself with soap and dance outside!

Needless to say, by the time I returned home yesterday, I resolved to live in the treehouse. Change is necessary. I can no longer live another day in limbo. If Joey persuaded Marty from beyond the grave to build me the treehouse, then this must be Joey's way to help me escape my father and Irving. The baby is gone. I have no loyalty to any family now.

After a shower, I dress and head for the garage. There is a home store now too far from the neighborhood. I should go there for linens and the like.

Driving becomes painful as I wean myself off the pain killers. Part of me questions whether I can make the quarter mile hike to the treehouse on a daily basis for awhile. Then again, my body will experience apathy if I remain stagnant. Exercise never harmed anyone.

The moment I walk into the home store, I become immediately overwhelmed with its vastness. I never set up a household on my own. My marital household was handed down to me from Father. The moment Irving and I said "I do'" he gave us the key. He created his own bachelor pad nearby. I have never been invited, but Irving has gone a dozen times for "intellectual retreats." I am not young enough to attend.

Instead of ruminating on my bitterness towards Irving and my father, I ought to be gathering necessities for my new life. Maybe I should have made a list before heading out. Too late now.

With winter around the corner, blankets are a priority. I head over to bedding. I could use a thick down comforter and a few fleece blankets. There are so many colors, how am I to decide? I can start by vetoing the earth tone colors. I spent by childhood enduring my parents' preferred palette of tan and beige. Am I too old to indulge in my childhood fantasies of decorating a household with vivid pinks, purples, and blues?

My phone vibrates loudly in my purse. I pull it out. Dr. Kroll is calling.

"Hello," I answer.

"Ms. Palavar? This is Dr. Joseph Kroll. I am calling to ask you if you are open to moving up your appointment today? Something came up for the afternoon I need to attend to. I have a spot available during the next two hours."

I forgot about my appointment with Dr. Kroll. I can't be spending an hour sitting in his office as he interrogates me. I have preparations to make.

"We can reschedule if you like," I suggest.

"I believe in keeping my appointments. If possible, I can see you within the hour."

"Sure," I comply. "I am out and about anyways."

"Great, I'll see you soon."

Dr. Kroll hangs up without formality. I quickly grab a blue comforter and pink and purple blankets. As I wait in the checkout line, I buy compost trash bags. I won't have the luxury of a garbage disposal anymore.

The cashier is ready to ring my purchases. To my surprise, my total is $120.98. I didn't think my blankets were extravagant. There are many things I still need to buy. I pull out my credit card fearing the I created enough debt to alert Irving.

The bags are troublesome to carry to the parking lot. Now I question whether I'll be able to bring them to my home in the woods. I'll think about it more while I drive to Dr.Kroll's office.

Dr. Kroll is pacing. It seems rather odd for a psychologist to appear nervous. After watching him for five minutes, I say, "If you need to address your matter now, we can reschedule our appointment for another day."

"No. No, there is something I particularly want to ask you. I just don't know how."

"Ask in any matter you see fit," I suggest aloud, finishing in my head, *you are the psychologist after all.*

Dr. Kroll sits down. He crosses and uncrossed his legs five times until he plants both feet to the ground.

"I want to ask you about the concept of 'enough .' You said that you believe you were not enough for your husband and father. I want to know what you think would be enough for them."

Ugh. Not this topic again. I just wish Dr. Kroll will give his blasé suggestions for my improvement. I can fix whatever he deems as my insufficiencies, and we both can just move on. Can't he just tell me what I lack? A smart man like him must know my inadequacies.

"I don't me their high intellectual standards," I answer.

"Which are?"

He pauses. He expects me to answer a rhetorical question. I heard psychologists could be weird. Dr. Kroll is downright absurd. With a lift of his eyebrow, he indicates he waits for a response. I shrug.

"I don't know. You're the intellectual elite. I was hoping you will tell me."

Dr. Kroll writes more in my file. "Are you saying that your father and husband desire a high level of cognitive function in a mate?"

"Yes," I answer, "Or maybe not. Hard to say. My mother was smart, but my father loathed her."

"Is your mother alive?"

"I'm not sure."

"How are you not sure?"

"I haven't seen her since my parents divorced! Are we going to stick to a consistent theme?"

Dr. Kroll writes more. "In psychology, randomness is consistent. Yet, I think I touched a nerve mentioning your mother. We can explore her situation further during another session. What I intended for this meeting was to explore how you remain connected to your family despite your feelings of unworthiness."

Now come the dreaded moment of truth that occurs in therapy. I planned to slip into my new life in the woods quietly. If I tell Dr. Kroll, he may alert someone. Lying my way out of the situation won't work either. I know from experience. Despite being hopeless in providing actual help, therapists are keen to sniff out a lie.

"I'm leaving Irving."

Dr. Kroll sat upright. "When did you decide on that?"

"The other day. An opportunity presented itself."

"I see. How did your husband take the news?"

"I haven't told him."

Dr. Kroll says nothing as he writes in my file. I won't say anything without a prompt. Dr. Kroll stares at the file quizzically. Finally, he speaks.

"You have never lived alone."

"Now is the time."

Dr.Kroll stares at me. He tries to hide an emotion. Which one, I can't decipher. He taps the top of his pen, shuts my file, and places it on his lap.

"Have you thought this through?"

"All but the cost," I answer. "I went to a home store and spent over a hundred dollars on blankets. I need more necessities, but I can't rack up too much debt. That would alert Irving something's amiss. I rather slip away quietly."

"I take it you intend to slip away soon."

"It's vital for me."

"How so?"

I sigh. "For the last twenty-some years, I've lived my life scrutinized in a hamster wheel. My only cause for my craziness was that I loved a boy who died. I've spent my life as a surrogate to a father I loathe and a husband I'm indifferent to, so they can be married to each other. I'm thirty-eight and never lived life for myself. If I express my desires, I will be bullied to maintain the status quo. Don't tell me I don't know that. I do."

Dr. Kroll stands up and opens the door.

"I guess I should let you go and continue your new journey."

I get up with a meek "thank you " escaping my lips. Dr. Kroll nods at me as I walk out the door.

As I walk down the hall, I hear, "Marion."

Turning around, I see Dr. Kroll looking out his office.

"Thrift stores should have everything you need. The ARC Value Village isn't too far from here. Otherwise, there is the Salvation Army off of 35W. Heck, every suburb has a Goodwill. You can get plenty of stuff without racking up the debt as you say."

"Thank you, Dr.Kroll."

I walk to my car feeling odd. I can't shake the sense that Dr. Kroll felt defeated towards the end of the session. It's like he didn't want me to leave Father and Irving but he had no choice. I shake my head. How I perceive Dr.Kroll to feel isn't my concern. I have important matters at hand. I get into my car and drive to the nearest thrift store.

14

Needless to say, when Joey died, Father saw mourning him a waste of energy and mental resources. He insisted I attend school the next day. Mother overrode him.

"She's missed so much school already. Why force her to go when her heart is breaking?"

"Because she has important matters to attend to."

My parents had many conversations about me around me. I sat amongst them as their words evaporated in my ears. Grief muted all my senses. I saw fog. The food I barely ate tasted like nothing. The only sensation I felt was cold, and I didn't care.

"I know you don't understand stand that ins and outs of young love, being that you never experienced it yourself," Mother explained. "A break up alone is devastating. Joey is dead. She is going to need a lot of care and understanding to get through her grief."

"I had a logical mind in my youth," Father remarked, "I didn't bother thinking of trivial pursuits such as dating."

"Tell yourself whatever you want. Maybe it will come true."

"I don't..."

"You've spent the majority of your forties sowing the wild oats you didn't sow as a teenager. You wouldn't be doing that now if dating didn't matter to you. Just go to work. I'll stay here with Marion."

I can't recall the string of days I spent in bed. One day Mother walked into my room with my black dress. Previously I wore it to the symphony. I knew it's purpose that day at a glance. I covered my head with my blankets.

"It would help you get closure if you attend the memorial service."

"I'm not ready to see his body."

"You'll never be truly ready to see his body," Mother responded. "It is a memorial service, anyhow. Memorial services often mean you will not see the body."

I peaked from the covers. "If there isn't a body, where's Joey?"

"I don't know," Mother answered. "The obituary didn't specify the cause of death."

I plopped my head onto the mattress. The covers lifted from my head. Mother led me into the shower. I stood underneath the falling water with my face lifted towards the facet. A stream of water entered my nose. I started sputtering. Despite the irritation, I lifted my nose towards the faucet again. Mother knocked on the door.

"Marion, you are going to be late."

I think I ignored her pleas. I may have blocked the memory of her barging into the shower to wash me. How I got dressed and arrived at Joey's memorial service is a blur.

To be honest, Mother and I didn't get to the actual service. The reception line was long. At the end was Joey's mom. I never met her during Joey's life. She knew me. "Bitch!"

"Excuse you?" Mother exclaimed.

Despite being a petite woman, Joey's mom had a commanding presence. She stood up and pointed a skinny finger towards me.

"She is the reason Joey's dead!"

Mother quickly defended me. "I don't see how this is Marion's fault. She gave Joey shelter and the means to survive after you chose your husband over your own son. If you sided with your child as you should have, none of this would ever have happened."

Joey's mother pointed to the door. "Get out!"

Mother led me out the door to the soundtrack of murmurs. I continued to walk towards the car. It was locked. I just stood there. The sun was out. The sky was blue. It meant nothing to me. All joy evaporated from my world. Some people enter your life and fill it with color and light. Once they leave, you stand in a cold shadow. Joey's absence forever cast a looming shadow everywhere I went. Because he opened my eyes to a world of love, I no longer wanted to live in a world devoid of it.

The click of the car locks singled mother's arrival. Once we got into the car, Mother handed me a box with a small cross charm glued on it.

"A boy was calling for you as you walked away. He thought you should have this."

I opened the box. It was nothing but gray powder. My love reduced to ashes. I only had a bit of him. If it weren't for the scruples of one of his friends, I wouldn't even have that. My love, my own, now was divided among other "true loves."

Mother drove me home in silence. She knew better than to say things like, "He's in a better place" or "You'll find another love." She gave me what I needed the most, space and time to grieve. If my father gave me the same, maybe what unfolded would never have transpired.

We found Father sitting at the kitchen table when we returned home. He welcomed us with a cold stare.

"She missed school again?"

Mother waved her hand. "Don't start with us. Joey's memorial service was today. His mother wasn't exactly a gracious host."

"Why do you keep enabling this nonsense?"

Mother nudged me to my room. "Go lay down, Marion. You had a rough day."

"No!" Father shouted. "She is going to change her clothes and come out here. She has a month of homework to do in one day."

"This is all too much for her," Mother pleded.

Father grabbed my arm and threw me into my room. My face hit the wall. He shut the door hitting Mother's face. She started pounding on the door. I cried.

2

"It's time to stop the hysteria and get a grip. That boy didn't love you. You know how I know that? Because I don't love you. How can I? You've given me nothing to be proud about. You're average. You have made no accomplishments whatsoever and you are about to flunk the eleventh grade. I can do without the embarrassment! You're pathetic like your mother."

He inched closer to me. I closed my eyes. He didn't hit me. Instead, he used his most powerful weapon, his words.

"You're nothing. You will never be anything until you bend to my will. Now get dress and wipe your pathetic tears..."

"Mitchel! Enough!"

Mother stood in the open door frame. "You need to leave."

He left.

Mother and I spent the rest of the night sitting on the couch. We pretended to watch a news station. Eventually, I conceded to my tiredness and went to bed. Mother kissed me and said goodnight.

I could hear the hum of the television from my bedroom. It started to lull me to sleep. The moment I drifted off, the garage door awoke me. My father's footsteps followed. Then I heard the television click off.

"You didn't have to come back," I heard my mother say. "In fact, we wished you wouldn't."

"I have a right to be in this house," Father replied. "I paid for half of the mortgage."

"Paying half of the mortgage doesn't make up for the destruction you brought into this house. The only peace we feel is when you leave. I must be the first woman who is happy that her husband is practically a pedophile."

"You shouldn't be alluding to my activities being anything illegal. You are the only person who partakes in criminal activity. In fact, I am surprised

I don't smell your illicit pleasure now."

"I have to be present for Marion," Mother answered flatly.

"When are you ever present?" Father asked. "I talk to you. I profess to you. You just stare at me blankly in your dreamland with your sweet grass warriors and mythical shaman."

"I think it's best for Marion and me to stay with my mother for awhile. We need time and space."

"The hell you are!" Father yelled. "Marion is my daughter. She is a representation of me. It is about time she stops being coddled and is made to live up to her potential. I am not going to have her go with you and be another drug using Indian cliche."

"She needs love. You aren't capable, Mitchel. You're not."

Mother started to cry.

I heard Father groan an inaudible threat. Mother followed with "You would be that cruel."

The house grew quiet. I heard heavy footsteps go downstairs while a door in the hallway closed. Soon the smell of sweet grass wafted into my room. The only sound I heard was my shaky breath. I loathed it. It was time to end it. I grabbed my robe and left. I didn't bother with shoes. I didn't see the point of them getting wet. After I completed suicide, my parents could donate them to charity.

The air was misty. The grass was dewy. The once skeletal trees became clothed in an abundance of green leaves. The moon reflected the every drop of moisture. Walking through the woods was walking through a dream. If death were an art, the creek would be its canvas. I only hoped that Joey died in blissful settings such as the creek. Did he die in the ocean he talked about so fondly? Was his death the result of his shenanigans in the desert? I approached the creek with a joyful heart knowing I would get to ask him soon.

My favorite part of learning about Virginia Wolfe was the end. She put rocks in her pockets and walked into the Atlantic Ocean to her death. The creek didn't have the depths of the ocean, but the melting snow made it impossible to see the rocky bottom. I filled my two pockets each with a rock large enough to fill it. I stepped into the creek. During the treacherous walk, I went into the storm sewer. Underneath the cement tube, I descended into the water.

I work up restraint to a hospital bed. Thus began a life I don't want to remember.

15

Following Dr. Kroll's advice to go to the thrift store proved fruitful. I found the rest of my necessities: a pot, a pan, a couple of plates, and some mugs. My greatest find was a pair of snow shoes. They will help me once it snows.

I go into the house and call out for Irving. Sometimes he comes home early in the afternoon. My calls echo throughout the house. I walk up the stairs. I grab seven outfits, a few pajamas, and the entire contents of my socks and underwear drawers. I dump everything in a kitchen garbage bag. I go to the bathroom and drop my toiletries in the bag and tie bag shut.

Father kept the old metal Radio Flyer wagon. The label is faded, and some of the red paint chipped away. In my attempt to pull it down from the loft, it crashes onto the cement floor. Wiggling the handle, I test to see if the axel is undamaged. Thankfully, wagons of my era were made to last.

I load the wagon with my things. I secure the pile with a couple of bungee cords I kept in my car. Off I go, away to my new home.

The sun starts to set. The brisk November air will prevent others from walking down the path. I can move in secret. Despite being twenty years since I escaped here at night, I navigate the path by instinct. Once I am at the bottom of the hill, I remove the bungees and move in by carrying one bag at a time. I finish before the sundown.

I am exhausted when I haul the final load to the hill. It takes all of my resolves to drag the empty wagon up the hill to store it in the closet. Once that is complete, I stand surrounded by the massive amount of my meager belongings. Now that the sun is down, my only source of light is a small decorative lamp. It's cute white porcelain base, and rose color lamp shade doesn't provide ample lighting for the task at hand. C'est le vie. The only thing I have the energy for is to prepare for bed.

Rummaging through the trash bag, I pull a pair of pajamas and my toothbrush. I use the sink to brush my teeth despite Marty's advice about iodine tablets. I pull the blankets out and lay on the futon while it remains in the upright position.

The sun shining through the skylight wakes me. I lay in blissful disbelief. I actually live in trees. My phone vibrates. Looking at the home screen, I see it must have vibrated throughout the night. I see Irving called ten times and sent five texts inquiring about my whereabouts. I also see from the time on the clock that I have two hours until work.

I gather an outfit and my shower necessities. I realize I don't have any things suitable to carry them in. Looking around, I see the irony in my dilemma. Plastic bags litter the floor around me. I take the ARC bag that contains my mugs and empty it on the table. The plastic bag will serve as my tote until I return to the ARC after work.

The early morning walk is refreshing. The crisp breeze wakes up my body, prompting a brisk walk. I make it to the garage with only a slight pain from the accident. After punching in the code on the keypad, the garage door opens. I dash into my car and zoom out the garage. I know I am reckless. The moment I turn onto the street, I catch a glimpse of Irving's head popping out of the house as the garage door shuts.

"Marion? You made it," a stunned Jessica Hank says upon my arrival.

"Yes, I have," I retort.

I roll my eyes as I sit in my cubicle. Jessica Hank wouldn't care about my attendance at work unless she has been talking to my husband. Her loud typing indicated she was chatting online with him. Five minutes later, I see him walking up the stairs through our office window. I get up to go to the restroom. Passing Jessica's desk, I say, "Your coffee date is here."

My coworkers must think I have the tiniest bladder. I went to the restroom once an hour to avoid Irving and Father. I shave fifteen minutes from the end of my shift to park my car at the house before Irving comes home. From the car, I sprint until I am cover by the safety of the trees. I limp the rest of the way home.

Now the sun has set. I wish that I went back to the ARC as intended. I could have bought some books to keep me occupied. Marty didn't configure the treehouse with wifi. Irving selected the cellular plan with limited data under the assumption that we never venture far from a wifi signal. With my limited connectivity, I can go on Amazon's website and order a couple of books. Now that I live alone, I gift myself an adult coloring book. Irving and Father mocked people purchasing adult coloring books. They believed ones who bought them were stuck in a juvenile mindset with a mediocre urge to color the world to their solipsistic ideas. Considering that Irving and Father are solipsists themselves, I roll my eyes recalling that comment.

Rain taps the sunroof. Looking up, I can make out small puddles above me. During my hospitalized days, rain was my only effective sedative. After weeks of insomnia, a good rain lulled me to sleep. The knowledge of being safe indoors as the sky fell upon the earth gave me security. Now I feel myself drifting off. A crash of thunder jolts me into consciousness. I quickly change into pajamas and burrow underneath my blankets.

I am startled awake by thunder clapping around the treehouse. Lightning brightens the cloudy white sky. I'm blinded as I peer out of my blankets. I pull the sheets over my head. Wind whips pass the treehouse with a whistling roar. Thunder echoes around me. Despite knowing my walls are insulated with rubber tires, I feel small and vulnerable.

The winds die down. I can hear my heart thump in my chest. I feel a light pressure on my back. In reaction, my limbs tuck themselves underneath my torso.

"The rain has stopped, Marion." I hear a familiar voice. "There was nothing to be scared of."

I peek out from the colony of covers. Illuminated by lightning, Joey stands at the foot of my bed.

16

He looks like the man I saw in heaven. Joey stands suspended in front of me. I reach out for him. My hands go through the chilled mass of air that makes his being. Joey moves into my body. With a sudden wave of warmth, I'm asleep.

I wake up late and alone. I quickly gather my clothes and run out of the treehouse. Thankfully I see Irving's car drive down the street through the trees. I quick run into the house and take a five-minute shower. I grab a granola bar to eat in the car. Irving left a half pot of coffee. It's still warm. I pour it into one of the many Nicollet travel mugs we possess.

It is registration time. I get to work in a booth all day. I run into it a minute before the partition gets raised. It's a long day. My boss buys my team lunch to eat in the booths and breaks us for ten minutes to use the restroom. Father and Irving come around to witness proof of my life. Both leave after a minute every time. Irving passes with a tender gaze. Father stands a yard away from the booths looking annoyed.

The registration booth keeps me at Nicollet into the evening. I check my desk to see if my order got delivered today. It has!

Irving left work hours ago. To avoid interacting with him, I park my car at the parking lot near Joey's old apartment. He stands in the clearing waiting for me. His hair is long, and he has that beard. He smiles as I walk down the path with my box in hand.

"You're bold," I said as we walk down the path together.

"How so?"

"Just by waiting in the open like that," I say, "what if somebody sees you?"

"Few can," Joey replies. "And those that do would think I am another spirit lost in the woods. The only one who is bold is you. You are talking to the dead."

"You're not dead, Joey. You're bodily challenged."

"Is that so," he chuckles.

"You stand more alive than me," I remark. "I feel I'm a soulless body walking around. Together, you and I can make up one living person."

Joey points me to a bridge. We walk over. I recognize it as the bridge where we took our prom photo It was also the bridge over the storm sewer where I attempted to take my life. We lean over the bridge with the box resting on the rail. Down yonder, I can see the stretch of the creek I saw in heaven. Absence from the view are the colorful leaves and the crystal frost over the rock.

"When I saw you in heaven," I say with a crack in my voice, "I believe that was the first time I felt alive since you died."

I feel warmth across my chest. Looking down, I see Joey wrapping his arms around me. We stand still watching the creek run underneath us. The sunset that mutes the colors of woods becomes the twilight that turns the trees to shadows. We have to proceed home before it's dark.

"You say there other spirits in these woods?"

"A few."

"Are they around here now?"

"Yes."

"How come I can't see them but see you?"

"They are souls that don't matter to you."

"You matter to me. Why am I only seeing you now?"

"Because you need me now."

I stop and stare at him. He glows under the darkening sky. His beauty doesn't ease my temperament.

"I needed you twenty years ago."

"Marion."

I continue to walk. I know Joey thinks he has the perfect answer. It's an answer I don't want to hear. It's not perfect. It will be an answer that suited his needs and never mine. I have heard too many such answers from men who thought they knew best.

"I needed you twenty years ago. There is no excuse. You can go now."

"Marion, you just weren't in the right frame of mind..."

My hand goes up. Joey is silent. He fades, and I proceed home.

I know my past. I attempted suicide. Forever I am referred to as a girl who just can't hack life. I've since learned to coast through my existence. Even that is not good enough for the people in my life. They want me to feel fulfilled as their doormat. In his life, Joey was my partner. We planned our life together. Heck, during our journey to Arizona I was the bossy one. He never berated me for taking control. How could I live on without an understanding person? Ironically, in death, Joey takes liberties in determining my fate.

I make it to the bottom of the hill. I notice a clump of sticks against the tree adjacent to the treehouse. The cluster becomes a mountain as I ascend the hill. Once I am at the top, I go to examine the new structure. There is an opening large enough for me to enter. Peering in, I see a haphazard wooden structure. I venture inside that see there is a hole on top of the structure. I now have an outhouse.

Chuckling to myself, I enter the treehouse. Joey stands by the table. The lamp is on.

"I must have left the light on," I say.

"No," Joey answered, "I turned it on."

"Thank you," I reply, "Now go."

I take off my coat and open my box. I sit on the couch with one of the books I ordered. Joey should get the idea he is unwelcome.

He doesn't.

"When you first attempted to end your life, I was there. I cheered you on. I stood on the rocks waiting for your spirit to emerge. When your dad arrived, I tried to throw stones. My death was too new. I didn't possess the strength. I never stop wanting us to be together."

I put my book down.

"You still haven't explained yourself."

"What can I say that will satisfy you? Marion, I have died. You have not. The afterlife is complicated. When I passed, I got questions with no answers. I have learned peace is accepting there will never be answers."

"Such as the reason for your death?"

"Yes."

"How did you die?"

"That is a question for another time."

"This is my house," I remark, "I demand an answer."

The lamp turns off. Joey stands before me in as an opaque white mist. The darkness solidifies his form. He glares at me.

"You sit in the house I built."

As fearsome as Joey stands, I will not play into his intent. Gathering all of my resolves, I rise from the couch and turn the lamps on. Joey is colorfully translucent.

"It will take more than parlor tricks to freighter me."

I return to the couch. Joey softly stares at me with sadness.

"You do not realize the bravery you've gained in your life. Have you died when you intended, you would not have the gumption you have now."

"A small consolation prize," I comment.

Joey stares at me with sadness.

"Death is limited liberation, Marion. I am free from bodily and emotional pain. I cannot participate in this world. I float and observe. The inability to contribute to humanity is insanity. I can see all, but I can't tell a human what they are missing. You, Marion, can dream, plan, set your life in motion. You aren't powerless as I."

"You can appear and disappear from my life when you please," I point out. "That seems very powerful to me."

Joey moves over to me. He places his hand on my face.

"Do you feel anything?" he asks.

"Warm air," I say.

Joey pulls away.

"I cannot touch you the way you need to be touch. I cannot be a romantic partner. All I can do is watch you."

"Why are you here?"

Joey turns away. "To stop you from doing what I want you to do the most."

Joey walks through the wall. I sit alone. Joey wants me to die so we can be reunited. Thankfully, he's left. I don't have the heart to tell him I have no intention of dying now.

17

"Tell me about your mother."

I sit at another session with Dr. Kroll. I didn't dread coming here today as I normally do. I want to explore my feelings about the conversation I had with Joey last night. I even figured out how to broach the topic without seeming delusional. As every therapist before him, Dr. Kroll has his own agenda.

"There isn't much to say about her," I answer, "haven't seen her in twenty-one years."

"Not at all?"

"Nope."

Dr. Kroll crosses his legs. "Why do you think that is?"

"My parents divorced during my second hospitalization. Her ceasing contact with me must have been a condition of the divorce."

"Have you ever attempted to contact her?"

"I wouldn't know how."

Dr. Kroll lists various forms of social media. I don't even have a Facebook account. There had been a time that I search her under Irving's LinkIn account. I couldn't find her.

"Perhaps you have no interest in finding her," Dr. Kroll remarks, " You twisting your face is your tell. You're disinterested."

"What would I say to her?" I respond. "Why are we talking about her? She wasn't the cause of my suicidal ideation."

"Mothers just don't leave their children, Marion," Dr. Kroll remarks, "especially when they are in crisis."

Dr. Kroll waits for my reaction. I stare at anything else. Dr. Kroll's office has limited distractions. Other therapists had plush pillows to hug, plastic toys to fidget with, or a tiny sand garden with a little rake to trace through. All I have is the arm of my chair to dig my nails into. Dr. Kroll watches as my nails nick the wooden arms.

"Marion, I don't allow avoidance. My goal as your therapist is to free you from your pain. The only path to freedom is to confront the pain. You do yourself no favors diverting the conversation."

"The topic of my mother hasn't brought me pain. I haven't thought of her that much until you brought her up," I reply. "I did have a dream the other night I wanted to discuss with you."

"I'm not a psychoanalyst of dreams, Marion. I practice legitimate therapies."

The irony is that I am going to speak about an actual event that occurred with my dead lover. To stay out of the hospital, I have to lie and say it was a dream.

"I think the dream reflects my growth."

Dr. Kroll sighs, "All right, I'll bite."

I draw a breath. I felt so confident entering this appointment, now, as I look at Dr. Kroll's expectant face I am losing my nerve. I realize I will not wow him like I thought I would.

"Well, Marion..."

"I had dreams that Joey visits me."

"As a ghost?"

"Yes. Yesterday, Joey confessed that he was with me during my suicide attempts. He wanted me to complete them so we'd be reunited. But, I realize I don't want to die. Not now."

Dr. Kroll relaxes his face. He's not overwhelmed by the revelation, but he's not passing it off as avoidance.

"Considering the love you claimed for this Joey, that is growth. Why do you think you don't want to attempt suicide again?"

"Maybe it is my new found dwelling?" I suggest. "It is the only change in my life."

"Sometimes a change in scenery shifts one's paradigm. I must confess, I've been curious about where you live now."

"It's a bit out of the ordinary," I say.

The blessed click of the timer occurs. I draw a grateful breath.

"Our time is up," Dr. Kroll says. "We will meet in two weeks time. Enjoy your Thanksgiving."

My face must have given a flash of confusion. Dr. Kroll quickly followed with, "It's next week."

"Yes, it is," I say. "Happy Thanksgiving to you as well."

I try not to race out of Dr. Kroll's office; but, I certainly don't dawdle. I put my coat on while walking down the hallway. Finally, the cold bursts of late autumn air greet me as I go to my car.

The morning frost partially remains on the fallen leaves. Snow will be falling soon. The walk from my car to the treehouse is arduously cold. I need to go back to the thrift shops to look for long underwear for the winter.

Reaching the hill, I see the familiar portly shape of Marty. We wave to one another as I climb the hill. Marty walks over to steady me as I reach the top.

"You're still in Minnesota," I say as he helps me up the hill.

"Not by choice," Marty replies, "My project got delayed. One of my suppliers is on strike. I have to stay here so I can get back to work the moment the nonsense ends."

I lean against a tree. As I wean myself from the pain killers, my walks leave me winded.

"Would you like to come inside?"

"I would, but the sun is going down. I don't know these woods well. I just wanted to see how you were doing and see how the outhouse was holding up."

"Thank you for assembling that," I said.

"My pleasure," Marty says as motions me to the outhouse. "I had a strange dream that Joey came to my hotel room and told me you lived here. I figured I'd checked things out. It took me an entire day to find branches and get them to fit together."

"It sure will beat using a bucket," I say.

Marty points into the outhouse. On the stool sat a package of gray toilet paper.

"To minimize the environmental impact, you are going to need to use unbleached, biodegradable toilet paper. Now, the snow is going to reduce the smell. The summer heat might make the woods stink to high heaven. You may want to buy some sand or some kind of dirt to get rid of the smell."

"Thank you. I'll keep that in mind."

Marty walks me to my door. "May I ask you a personal question?"

"Ah, sure?"

"What are you going to do in January?" Marty asks. "Doesn't the temperature drop to below zero up here?"

I feel myself blushing. Bodily functions are a taboo topic in my family. In fact, I had to train myself to make bowel movements when Irving was away. Thankfully, he was an absentee husband.

"I guess I'll just use a bucket," I chuckle.

Marty laughs then says, "I best be going. You have a great night."

I watch Marty go down the hill. I follow him from the top. As he is about to reach the bottom, I gain my nerve to shout, "Marty! May I ask you a personal question?"

Marty stops and turns around. "Sure!"

"What are you doing for Thanksgiving?"

"Sit in my hotel room, I guess."

"Would you like to come here for dinner?"

"I'd love too!"

Marty waves then head east. I go inside the treehouse. I feel a familiar spark of giddiness. It's surprising. Marty is only a friend.

I spent the majority of my weekend planning a simple Thanksgiving menu and the logistics of getting the food to the treehouse. My dilemma didn't have a resolution by the time I went to work on Monday.

Classes were not in session the week of Thanksgiving. Registration administrators still had to come to work. There was a lot to be done given that many students change their minds at the last minute. The three days before Thanksgiving is spent weeding through student emails while answering panic phone calls. Despite knowing I am up for a week of hard work, I am grateful for one thing: not having to risk running into Father or Irving. Or so I thought.

"Have you enjoyed your time of insolence?"

Father's voice sends shivers up my spine. He traps me before I make it to my desk. Still, I have to put on a brave face. I turn to face the heart of stone who ruled my life for decades. He stands firmly.

"Yes, Father, very much so."

"End it."

"End what?"

"Your childish rebellion. It stops today."

"There is no rebellion," I explain. "I am only taking charge of my life."

Father snorts. With that, I turn and head for my office.

"The plane takes off at six pm. I expect you at the airport at four thirty."

The family trip to Vermont, how I loathe it. Visiting Father's side of the family was horrid enough. At first, it was mockery about my mother's Native American heritage. Once she left, I endured ridicule over my mental illness. Once Irving got added to the familial mix, I divided my time between being ridiculed by my family and ignored by his. For once, I have another option this year.

"I won't be leaving with the two of you today," I say, "I have work. You know that."

Father heads to the direction of my desk. "I'll speak to your supervisor. She should know of your delicate health."

"My health is only a concern of yours when it's convenient," I argue. "Even then, your concern is about appearance. God forbid if your colleagues figure out the daughter you raised isn't well adjusted."

Father shakes his head. "Don't worry, Marion. My colleagues are well aware of the fact. They have children who succeed in politics, law, the arts, or follow their paths in academia. They see you in the registration office and wonder what went wrong with you. Now, you come to work, but you don't come home. How am I to explain to my sister that you aren't celebrating Thanksgiving with us?"

"That I received a better opportunity," I answer, "so I took it. Now, I have work to do! Enjoy your trip and give Irving my best."

Father mutters a reply. I can't hear it. If I turn around and ask him to repeat his insults, I'd only be playing his game. As long as I don't interact with him, he can't hurt me. It's sad that the man I'd feared the most was the man that tradition dictated me to trust. I choose not to dwell on that. Instead, I grow in the strength I gain from walking away from him.

18

Assured that Irving went to Vermont with Father, I attempt to enter the house the day following Father's confrontation. I punch in the code to the garage door. The lights behind the punch pad glow red. I punch the code again. I get a red light. This is ridiculous! My family used the same code since my parents purchased a combination garage door opener. Mother selected the birthday of their only child. I certainly never forgot that date!

I go to the front door. I still have the house keys. Approaching the door, I notice a small disc above the doorbell. I stop and squint. It's what I think it is. Irving installed a camera for the front door, most likely at Father's behest. I've seen commercials and know that I will appear on video on Irving's phone if I get any closer.

I walk back to the treehouse. My plan for Thanksgiving with Marty was to cook our dinner at the house and serve it at the treehouse. If the day brought warm weather, we could eat on a park bench near the creek. So much for that idea.

Irving's doorbell camera can't deter me. All one needs to do is type a few words on the internet, and the desired information pops up. I type "Stove Top Thanksgiving" on my phone's browser. Five recipes pop up. I can make mashed potatoes, sweet potatoes, and green beans. I'll skip the Brussels sprouts. I prefer Marty isn't privy to the terrible gastric effects I endure after consuming them.

The day before I go to the grocery store. Despite the last minute shopping, I find everything thing I need for our rustic Thanksgiving meal. At the deli, I buy slices of cooked turkey breast. I can sear them in a pan. If the weather is nice enough, we could heat them over a bonfire! I leave the store confident in my plan.

My confidence evaporates over the stove as I fail to execute my recipes.

The sauce for the green beans doesn't thicken. The butter evaporates in the pan. Somehow my attempt to make the sweet potatoes' marshmallow glaze causes the stove to catch fire!

Thankfully, Marty enters at the formation of the blaze. He extinguishes the flames in seconds. Unfortunately, the only method of operation is my hundred dollar comforter. A black ash circle decorated the bright blue bedding.

"Sorry about that," he says, "I'll buy you a new one."

I shake my head. "It was my own carelessness. Besides, I paid a ridiculous amount of money for that. The ashes give it character."

"It sure does" Marty chuckles.

Marty bends down to pick up a mess of green stems and white petals. He hands me the haphazard bouquet on one knee. "For you."

"Thank you."

Marty reaches his hand out to me. I help steady him as he rises from the floor.

"I'm afraid dinner didn't turn out the way I hoped."

"That's alright. This set up still beats sitting in my hotel room alone eating whatever I could find at the gas station. You know, because all the restaurants are closed."

Not all the restaurants are closed. There was one place my mother's family went to ignore Thanksgiving.

"Ever been curious about how the Native Americans celebrate Thanksgiving?"

Marty gives me an awkward look. "I don't talk politics. Especially racial politics because I never know how to say the right thing."

I grab my coat. "I know a restaurant that is open."

****

"This is not a restaurant!" Marty exclaims, "This is a palace."

Marty and I are at Wana Yi Lake Casino. It stands on sovereign Dakota land. Over the years it has become the event center south of the Twin Cities. One of the amenities Wana Yi Lake offers is the best buffet in the state.

We walk the long stretching hallway. Marty is easily distracted by the slot machines and televisions that advertise special concerts and bingo events. I have to nudge him every few seconds. When we get to the buffet, Marty stops in awe. Standing before him are aisles of fine foods from various cultures.

I pay our admission. Once we sit and order our sodas, Marty goes off and returns with three plates of food. I make my first trip to the salad bar. Marty has one plate cleared when I return to our table.

"This is great! You actually ate like this every Thanksgiving?"

"I wish."

Marty looks around. "You told me that this is how the Native Americans spent Thanksgiving, but I see everybody."

In Minnesota, we don't say such things; however, Marty is right. The Twin Cities is diverse. Every demographic is represented here tonight. Whereas I'd admonish anyone else who'd made such a comment, I find myself giggling at Marty.

"Everyone wants to escape their family on Thanksgiving. I'd wish I got the opportunity to come here growing up. We spent Thanksgiving trapped at my aunt's house in Vermont."

"Yeah, my father grew up not too far from here in Chicago. Thanksgiving was the time we celebrated with his family. We stayed in Anaheim on Christmas. My mom would help my grandma prepare the celebrations. Christmas was a big thing in our family."

He is sincere when he proclaims that Chicago isn't far from here. I suppose Minneapolis isn't far from Illinois compare to California. He has a realistic whimsy about him. I find myself getting lost in conversation with him. Not since Joey has an average conversation been captivating.

"Do you get to spend time with your family in Anaheim nowadays?"

"Well, now it is only my mom and I. Dad died a couple of years ago. Mom...she had a stroke. Dad...he just died from exhaustion. I'm an only child. The contracting work pays well. I got Mom in a nice facility. I am thinking about homesteading here in Minnesota. I've seen the assisted living facilities here. They're better than where Mom is at now. It would be good for her here."

"I am sorry to hear about your parents."

"It is what it is," Marty comments. "Parents are supposed to grow old. The unfortunate truth is that if you live life right, you will have to bury your parents."

I nod at the sad fact, not knowing a pithy reply. My silence becomes detrimental. Marty follows up with, "What about your parents?"

"I work at the community college my father teaches at," I answer, "I see him every weekday."

"What about your mother?"

Thankfully my plate is empty. I excuse myself and walk up to the buffet, loading my plate with more than I can eat. I head back once a have a suitable answer.

"Actually," I say sitting, "My mother grew up around here. My grandmother was part of the Dakota nation."

"Joey mentioned that," Marty answers as he eats a roll that fell off my plate.

"I came around here for pow-wows, but never to play. Do you gamble?"

"I went to Vegas once. I had fun, but spent way too much money."

"The night is young. Would you like to play the slots after dinner?"

"I'm more of a blackjack man, but sure."

125

We each go back to the buffet for a plate of dessert. Actually, Marty gets two. Then it's off to the casino. Marty insists we get drinks after we get a roll of quarters. We go to the bar in the middle of the sea of slot machines. Marty buys me a glass of merlot and a Jack and Coke for himself.

With drinks in hand, Marty and I walk down the aisles of slot machines. There were too many cutesy themes: Woodland, Nautical, and various pop culture machines. Marty stops in front of a GodFather machine.

"Heya, that's what I'm talking about," he says. "My favorite movie. It's a requirement for us Sicilian males to love this film."

I sit down at a Star Trek machine because it's next to Marty's machine.

"I think it is a requirement of all males to love 'The GodFather," I reply.

We mindlessly put quarters in a machine. I blow through my roll in ten minutes. Marty is up by ten bucks.

"Maybe I just need another drink?" I suggest.

"I'll be right here," Marty says.

I get lost on my way back to the bar. I find myself among the blackjack tables. It's the hazard of drinking after abstaining during the pregnancy. Nonetheless, I see another bar!

There are times I feel others are staring at me. Often, when I look, I see someone doing just that. At a blackjack table, there is a woman with long white hair staring at me. At first, I pay no heed to her. I proceed to the bar and get a screwdriver this time. I walk back to find Marty; my eyes lock onto the woman again.

"Hey, Marion!"

Marty emerges from the crowd. "I thought I lost you."

"I got myself lost."

Marty looks around. "Looks like you found the right place. I wanna play some blackjack!"

Marty grabs my hand and heads for the table where the woman stares at me. As we get closer, I realize she is one of the dealers.

"Five dollars a deal," she says. "Bills, no change."

"I guess I got to exchange some quarters!" He taps my bottom. "Save my spot, Dollface."

In a less than inebriated state, I would have given Marty the what for. Or would I? Marty is the classic dopey male stereotype, the type of guy who tries too hard. I'm finding him adorable.

The dealer is unimpressed. She gives Marty the stink eye as she shuffles the cards. Her attention to us is unnerving. I ought to go with Marty. Just when I resolve to leave, I hear a familiar voice say, "So, you decided to skip Vermont this year."

My mother's face barely aged in the last twenty years, except for the crow's feet around her eyes. She wore her waist length hair pulled up in a ponytail. Figures, I haven't thought of her for decades, and there she stands before me after Dr. Kroll inquires about her. It's as if he manifested her through the power of psychology. I shake my head at that lame thought.

"Where have you been?" I ask.

"Jail," Mother answers, "then Montana and Alaska before coming back here to take care of Grandma Larson."

"Grandma Larson?"

"She had cancer."

"Had?"

"She's passed."

Marty comes back with a fistful of bills. I feel the heat radiating from my skin as I watch Mother deal Marty three games. How could my grandmother pass and no one tell me? How could she go to Alaska and Montana while I wasted away with Father? All the feelings I suppressed in Dr. Kroll's office bubble over from my heart. Marty is losing another game.

"Honey," I say placing a hand on Marty's arm, "why don't we go before you lose all the winnings?"

"Sure. I guess my luck ran out."

We turn to leave.

"I live in Grandma Larson's trailer. It never moved. You can come by if you want."

"I think we should just let bygones be bygones," I reply.

I take Marty's hand. My boldness silences him. We walk through the maze of bars, tables and slot machines until we reach the aisle to the doorway. Finally, cold winter air greets us outside. We run to my car. Marty out runs me and stands by the driver seat.

"Marion, let me have the car keys."

19

Marty drives pass my exits for the parks of Miles Creek. When I see signs for the airport and Killebrew Drive, I realize that he's taking me to his hotel. Not just any hotel, Marty is staying at the Marriott attached to the Mall of America.

"You had a little too much to drink. If I try to walk you home, we'll just get lost in the woods."

Marty's voice is thick with concern. Seriously, I haven't drunk enough to be compromised. I don't feel like being alone. During the car ride, Marty proves to be an excellent companion for silence. I unbuckle my seatbelt and follow him out of the car.

My family didn't have vacations at hotels. We either rented a camper or stayed with relatives during our travels. Without having a point of reference, I found Marty's room grand. Considering he was hired by the Mall of America, he ought to be in a superior suite.

Marty opens a small refrigerator and pulls out a bottle of water. "I got cans of juice cocktails in there if you wanted that instead."

"Water is fine."

I sit on a couch. Marty rolls an office chair from the nearby desk to sit in front of me.

"You knew the lady dealing blackjack?"

"My mother."

Marty gives a surprised reply. "Your mother? It looked like you haven't seen her in a long time."

"My entire adult life."

"I don't understand. I remember Joey telling me that your mom was cool."

"Was being the operative word," I remark.

"Joey said you had troubles at home, but they were with your dad."

I sigh. "Joey was the balm that soothed my soul against the family bullshit. When he died, my family still sucked. He was the only person who understood me. His death is something I am still not over. You don't get over losing a person like Joey."

"I know," Marty replies, "especially given how he died."

"How did Joey die?"

"You don't know?"

Marty stares at me in disbelief. Then he looks down. I feel foolish. For twenty-one years, it didn't occur to me look up the means to Joey's demise. Being told he was killed sufficed. The tone of Marty's voice bugs me. Something amiss happened.

"Nobody elaborated," I explain. "I was the only told he died. Simple as that, I guess."

Marty shakes his head. "It isn't that simple. I rather not get into it."

Marty heads to the bedroom. He stops at the doorway. "You can take the bed. I'll sleep on the couch."

"Thank you."

I go to the bedroom. Marty calls out, "There is a spare toothbrush. You can use that. Feel free to use my toothpaste."

"I will. Thanks."

Shutting the door, I remove my clothes. There is a terry cloth robe with the hotel's monogram. I slip into it. I go to the bathroom and find the plastic wrapped toothbrush. I brush my teeth and head for bed.

The bed is vast. Despite covering myself with all the blankets, I still feel exposed. I am alone. I don't want to be. I don't have to be.

Marty is watching television in his underwear. His eyebrows shoot up when he sees me open the door.

"Marty? We can talk more if you like."

"I don't feel like talking, Marion. Sorry."

"I don't want to talk either, but..."

Marty waits for me to finish my sentence. I don't know what to say. "Howdy Stranger, let's sleep in the same bed," is too forward of a sentence. Therefore I stand in the doorway like an idiot. Marty turns off the television. He walks over to me.

"At least we agree on not talking," he says.

Marty walks to the right side of the bed. I follow to the left. Slowly we gravitate to the middle. It occurs naturally. Marty isn't Joey, but his gentle attentiveness comforts me. Irving lacks that quality in a lover. Marty finishes with a calm assurance. He rolls over, draping my arm around him. I close my eyes with the intention of sleeping peacefully.

The rising sun wakes me. I see an illuminated Joey when I open my eyes. I gasp his name.

"Joey?" Marty says with a start.

I don't think. I blurt, "Joey is here! I see him sometimes. I should have told you...."

"Joey is here?"

"Please don't think me as a psycho."

Marty looks towards the window. "If Joey is with us, so is my wife."

131

****

Marty drives me to the park in silence. I get out and wave him away. What is there that say? I see the ghost of his dead cousin. He has a dead wife. I never told him about Irving or my name changing to Palavar. I never intended to. Could it be we were just two desperate maniacs last night?

The sky is clear I walk through the woods in a fog of my own confusion. Joey: Why did he show up? Marty: Why didn't he tell me about being married? Irving: I just cheated on him. Shouldn't I feel guilty? I know the answer to the latter is a resounding no. There is a sadness to that fact. Worst, I feel that the person I've betrayed is my first loved whose death was twenty-one years ago.

I enter the treehouse to see Joey floating over the table as if he is sitting on it. His eyes were to the door when I enter, but he turns his head the moment I walk into the room.

"I am so sorry," I breathe.

Still looking away, Joey answers, "For what? You and Marty are humans. Humans need to touch each other. I can't fulfill that need. I'm a ghost."

But you are the love of my life? I shouldn't be with another.

Joey knows what I don't verbalize.

"This isn't the first time you been with a man since I passed, Marion. What is it about Marty that makes you feel guilty?"

"Irving is a means to ah....something. Marty is as you said, another human."

Joey looks at me with a gaze that pierces my heart. He floats over to me. The heat I became accustomed to in his presence becomes cold.

"Did you really love me, Marion, or was I just your sexual awakening?"

"I love you, Joey. How can you ask that?"

The room gets warmer as Joey backs away or my blood boils at his words. He looks at me wounded. I won't have it.

"Every girl you ever slept with claimed to be your true love when you died, girls you slept with when I loved you! You have the audacity to question my love for you, Joey Troli! You're right, Marty is human! I need another human. I certainly don't need a dead boyfriend reappearing twenty-one years after he left!"

"I know, Marion," Joey whispers, "I know."

"Marty doesn't seem like the man who'd sleep with women Willy Nilly," I continue. "He felt guilty about cheating on his dead wife..."

Joey interrupts me with laughter. The treehouse shakes. I grab the back of a chair for balance. Joey floats behind me. I feel his chilling breath as he whispers, "And you don't feel guilty about cheating on your living husband."

Joey leans in on me. All of a sudden, I am engulfed in his being. His voice vibrates through my entire being.

"You live here because of me. I died because of you."

I can't say the words I need to. I am paralyzed within Joey's soul.

I had nothing to do with your death! I love you! Kill me if it will make you happy! My life isn't a life.

Joey releases me. He looks at me, pleading for an apology. My knuckles are white from gripping the chair.

"I was afraid of you when I was alive, Marion. I was obsessed. All I wanted was to consume you, every bit of your being. I almost killed you now. That is not how love is or should be. That is the reason I stayed away. I should have stayed away."

"Don't you think of leaving," I croak. "Don't you dare, Joey Troli."

Joey heads to the door. "I have to. I've awakened you again, Marion. Instead of your passion, I awoke your anger. You'll provoke me again, and I may not have the restraint to release you, epecially if you beg I don't."

Joey walks through the door.

133

"Wait! You need to answer a question!"

Joey floats his disembodied head through the door. "What is that?"

"How did you die?"

Joey sighs. "Maybe you shouldn't let bygones be bygones with your mother. Goodbye, Marion."

The entire room went dark. I turn on the small lamp. There is nothing but little shadows. In the absence of Joey, the air is thick with loneliness.

20

My morning is spent laying on the futon staring through the skylight. The burdens from yesterday's revelations left me devoid of energy. Marty is a widower. Joey's torment could cause me harm. Neither will be coming around due to their scruples.

By noon, the sun shines through the skylight. I cover my head with the comforter to avoid blindness. The result is roasting in a fabric oven. I sweat badly enough to want a shower. Unfortunately, I have no means of obtaining one.

Maybe the cold air will freeze the sweat off of me. I open the door. The air is frigid. The earth is damp by melted frost. Winter is coming. Soon it will snow, and I may not have the means to leave. Yes, I realize I may be crazy for living in a treehouse in the middle of the woods with no bathroom.

Maybe you shouldn't let bygones be bygones.

Joey's voice alerts me to an available shower. I go inside and pack my bag then walk to my car.

By muscle memory, I get to my Grandmother's trailer. She lived only five minutes from the casino. I park the car in the woodland trailer park. Most of the trailers from my childhood still stand. I can see the decades' worth of wear and tear. I get out of the car, but I stand there.

Mom comes out wearing a knitted house coat with a mug of tea in her hands. She raises it towards me. "I can make you one of you come in."

I walk to the door. Mother holds it. There is no attempt for any affection. Maybe the stoic Scandinavian genes blossomed in her old age. Once inside I say, "I hoped I'd be allowed to use the shower.

Mother shakes her head. "You sound so English. Go ahead. It's at the end over there."

I walk where she pointed. The bathroom remains in the avocado color of Grandma Larson's time. I can faintly smell her lavender scent. The shower is cold despite having the faucet turned to the left. I make it quick. Mother uses generic drug store shampoo and soap. As pretentious as it sounds, I can feel a film linger on my skin.

I take a while to dress after my shower. When I mentioned letting bygones be bygones, I meant it. My previous numb existence after my parents' divorce became comfortable. Mourning Joey produced enough pain for a lifetime. Ignorance to my other family issues was bliss. Now I am going to listen to stories I never cared to hear, mostly for the purpose of self-preservation.

Mother is at her small table with her mug. She pushes a tea box towards me.

"Take your pick. I'll go put the kettle on."

Mother goes to a small stove and turns a dial. She opens up a cupboard. With her face hidden, she says, "What's happened to letting bygones be bygones?"

"I needed a shower."

Mother pulls a mug with a timber wolf printed on it. She turns to me with an unconvinced look.

"You have a shower at your house."

"Not really," I answer. "I moved into a minimalist dwelling a few weeks ago."

Mother arches her eyebrow. The kettle whistle. She pours water into the mug while I select cranberry tea from the tea box. She puts the mug in front of me.

"You live alone?"

"Yes."

Mother sits down on the chair across from me. "I am interested in how you manage to leave that overbearing father of yours."

Mother has some gall. She left me behind and thinks she has the right to know my life.

"Actually, I am interested in how you escaped him."

Mother ran her finger around the rim of her mug. It's black with the Dakota tribal crest printed on it. She's not going to answer right away. I bide my time. I look around the kitchen. It's made up of the repurposed wood a cousin used to make the cabinetry. The Native relics were minimal compared to my grandmother's days. Food and dishes are put away. That's also different from when Grandma Larson lived.

"You were told I left."

I look at Mother. "I wasn't told anything. You weren't there when I was released. You never came home. It's a simple concept to deduce."

"I didn't leave on my accord. He had me arrested."

That is the last thing I expected out of her mouth. Then she walks out of the room and returns with a canister and cigarette papers. How could I have questioned the last statement?

"Yet you still partake."

Mother rolls herself a doobie. "Your father damaged me as well. The anxiety developed during our marriage took a life of its own. You never saw how he punished me for standing up for you. I don't care to relive it now."

I grimace as she lights her blunt.

"Does this offend you?"

Considering there were legal medications for anxiety, yes I am offended. I am also offended realizing we could have gone to the trailer to live with Grandma Larson. The trailer park is on sovereign land where the state of Minnesota has no juristriction. He couldn't come after us without dealing with the Native government. Unlike most people, we have a safe haven!

"I think your marriage was a convenient excuse for the pot," I remark.

Mother drops her joint in her mug. She assumes that I will believe she ruined it; however, I know it is brewing in her mug. She'll drink it once I leave.

"I don't understand why he got you arrested when he lived with the knowledge of your activities for years," I comment.

Mother folds her arms on the table and gives an exasperated sigh.

"It was the divorce, duh! He wanted custody because he believed you needed electric shock therapy. I wanted to move you to a spiritual sanctuary. We had a row, and he banished from the hospital. The moment I lit my blunt that night, the police knocked on the door. Anonymous report I was told. Bull shit. He set it up. I lost everything because of him."

My father's underhanded deed disgusts me. Still, in the back of my mind come a nagging thought, "you brought this on yourself."

"At least you had something," I say. "Plus, you traveled to Alaska and Montana. Both are beautiful states."

"Eastern Montana isn't," Mother replies, "It's flat like North Dakota. Northern Alaska is desolate. I spent five years in prison. I lost my job. I went with some friends to find work. I got stuck working as a farm hand in both states. That is not want I earned a master's degree for."

We want the other to feel pity for our life. That isn't going to happen. My mother sees me as the reason for her disgraced life. I see her as the mother who abandoned me.

"So, did you just assume I died? Is that why you didn't bother to contact me from Alaska or Montana?"

"I wrote you letters the first year. I didn't get a reply."

"I never got them."

"He had a no contact order. I was presented with it upon my release. Don't you blame me. You were what, twenty-three when I left prison. You were an adult perfectly capable of contacting me yourself."

"Nobody told me where you were," I reply. "It's hard to initiate contact without knowing where to call."

"Grandma Larson's phone number never changed. You could have called her."

"Likewise."

With that, Mother has no blame to pass to me. I remain to finish my tea. It's good tea not to be wasted. Mother's face twist to her internal conflict. Should she kick me out or remain grateful we are in contact?

She breaks the silence with, "Your man seems nice."

"You know about Irving?"

"Irving? You were calling him Marty the other day."

"Oh, yes," I reply. "He's just a friend. Actually, he is Joey Troli's cousin. Do you remember my friend, Joey?"

Mother took a gulp of her tea. "You are in contact with the family?"

"Just him and only recently," I answer.

"You know, the family sued us for what your father did."

What did my father do? My eyebrows shoot up.

"He hired the bounty hunter who killed Joey."

"A bounty hunter?"

Mother pulls out a tobacco cigarette from her back pocket. She lights it and hands it to me. I sit frozen as it burns in my hand.

"Bet you thought I didn't know about your illegal habit," she snorts.

"Yes, your father was bound and determined to punish Joey for stealing your virginity. It was a stroke of luck for him that you didn't meet the age of consent in Arizona. He hired the bounty hunter to make Joey face the statutory rape charges."

My hands shake. Mother takes the cigarette from my hands and snuffs it out on a knot on the table.

"Bounty hunters don't kill people," I stammer.

Mother shrugs. "Joey wouldn't go without a fight. Unfortunately, he fought to the death. Your father placed a desirable bounty on his head. Joey was worth the savings bonds you stole."

I stand up. I need to go. Mother places her hand on my arm. I walk towards the door anyways.

"Marion, you shouldn't go off by yourself."

I turn to Mother. "The days when I jumped into the river are long gone."

Instead, I have rage. It forces me to remain awake and alive. The anger propels me to the old house and drive through the garage door. Age made the wood brittle. I crunch a big enough hole to walk through. Irving never locks the door into the house from the garage. I walk in and run downstairs. Father kept his old documents stored in his study. I fling all the files out until I find what I am looking for, the recipes from the bounty hunter. Joey appears in front of me. He nods.

"You're awake."

I toss it on the floor with the other papers and leave.

21

"He just hired the guy," Joey says, "he didn't tell the guy to kill me."

Joey stands with me over the bridge. November can spark unseasonably warms days. Today it is forty degrees. I've spent all day walking the along Miles Creek with the intent to calm my mind. Joey follows me. When no one is walking by us, we talk.

"Father set the bounty with my saving bonds. That amount would set off any overzealous hunter. It did. You're dead."

Joey walks through the rails and floats down to the creek. He stands on the water. He's been doing these things all day: walking through trees and floating over me. His intent is humor, but I am finding his tricks tiresome. I need to process. Joey, being the boy he is, does everything in his power to avoid a discussion. He motions me down. I shake my head. I am not getting wet.

"All is said and done," Joey says as he floats up to the rails. "Your father didn't kill me. The man who did went to prison. He got shived and died."

"Joey, Father wanted you out of my life permanently. Not only, he did achieve that, but he also got away with murder! He needs to pay!"

Joey wraps his arms around me from behind. He melts into my being. My breathing slows. His voice vibrates throughout my body.

"He is not worth it, Marion. Seeking revenge will only invite him back

141

into your life."

Joey's words are wise. They don't evaporate my anger. My father is a man of vice due to his dalliances with young students. True, my mother being a pothead and me the teenage runaway didn't make us people of strong moral fiber. I fail to see what right Father had to use actions against us while he carries on.

Joey starts seeping beneath my flesh and massages my inner spirit. That's his spiritual version of copping a feel.

"Will you stay on?" I ask

"What do you mean?"

"The only way I can remain calm is if you stay."

The sun sets into the golden reflection on the river. The blue sky illuminates over us. I took a film class in high school. Filmmakers call this time of day the magic hour. This moment is truly magical for reasons beyond the sun's placement in the sky. Without his body, Joey can enter into me until we become one. We stand overlooking the creek breathing in tandem. In the midst of the chaos, I have found my source of peace.

To remind us that we are in Minnesota, Mother Nature drops the thermostat down to ten degrees. I woke up shivering and staring at a white dome. I open the door to find three inches of snow covering the ground. Great. The roads will be a mess. I pack my bag. Thankfully, the weather only calls for heavy boots.

After showering and grabbing breakfast, I head upstairs. Irving stands at the bottom of the staircase. I walk pass him.

"We need to talk."

Without turning to face him, I reply, "We said all we were going to say the way Minnesotans do."

Irving is from Vermont, yet he is well practiced in the art of passive-aggressiveness. I hear a bemused chuckle and move on.

Snow falls off and on during the day. By the time my day is done, it is six inches deep. Snow falls into the tops of my boots and my socks. I need to go back to the thrift store to find snow pants.

Finally, I am home. Immediately I change clothes. I turn on the electric kettle and wrap one of the fleece blankets around me. I sit at the table with a coloring book.

There is a knock at the door. I drop my pencil. Is it Marty? Of Course, it is Marty! He is the only person who knows I am here. I run to the door and open the peep door. It isn't Marty. It's Irving!

"May I please come in?"

Marty made the peep door too big. Irving can see me on the other side. Begrudgingly, I open the door. Irving steps in. He wears his wool peacoat and his brown leather loafers which are now encrusted with snow. He doesn't have hats or gloves; just a ridiculous scarf Jessica Hank knitted him for a white elephant party.

"So this is where you live," Irving remarks, "a house for elves."

He smirks. I roll my eyes at his attempt crack a joke.

"Why are you here, Irving?"

Irving brushes the snow off his coat.

"We need to talk."

"As I mentioned at work, we communicated what we needed in our way."

Irving gives this exasperated sigh. I am not falling into line. After not being subjected to it for the past month, I find the sound of his sighs jarring. I sigh back, and he stares at me in surprise. I left him to live my life. What right does he have to intrude on my solitude?

"I'll rephrase," I retort, "Irving."

"Marion."

143

"How the hell did you find this place!"

Irving steps back with a palm out. He thinks I'm too hostile. What did he expect? No one likes an intruder.

Irving straightens his scarf. "You were coming to work but not coming home. One day we followed you."

"We? Please tell me you aren't talking about Father."

"I am," Irving answers. "Needless to say, we were shocked to find that this is where you disappeared to. Naturally, we assumed that this was a phase and you would return. On the plane, we were talking about your situation. We have decided that it is time for reason to take over. I am here to take you home."

"I am home."

Irving opens the closet. "Is this the only room?"

"I have an outhouse."

As Irving pokes around my closet, I feel Joey's warmth around me. I sense his amusement when Irving emerges from the closet. *Yes, Joey, that short, balding shit is the man I married.*

"It is going to snow, Marion. A blizzard is being predicted."

"We live in Minnesota," I comment, "we are overdue for snowfall."

"A foot of snow will fall tonight followed by the temperature dropping to single digits. You won't be able to survive."

"I've survived here for a month."

"You won't be able to leave here tomorrow," Irving remarks, "Everything will freeze. Come."

Joey wraps his spirit tighter. I pled with him, *scare him away! You are a ghost after all!*

Joey does nothing. Instead, Irving threats, "So God help me, Marion, if you do not leave with me, I'm calling your father!"

"Seriously, it's come to that?"

Irving nods. Joey evaporates. There's nothing to do but get my coat and snowshoes.

Irving is not the type to enjoy a moonlit walk, at least not with me. He walks at a brisk pace. The snow begins to fall again. Irving picks up the pace. If Joey walks with me, we'd be stopping a moment to admire the scenery. Irving wants to speed up the moments with me.

We're chilled to the bones as we approach home. Irving heads to his room, and I head to mine. All my fleece pants are at the treehouse. My only option is light cotton pajama pants I wear in the summer. I search my closet for a sweatshirt. The only one I found was a Bloomington Lincoln High School pullover.

I go out to the kitchen. Whenever we went to Vermont, we would purchase locally crafted alcohol. I don't see a bottle on the counter. I begin my search in the cupboards. I must be loud for Irving exits his room.

"What are you doing?"

"Looking for the apple bourbon you brought home," I answer.

"I didn't bring any."

"Come on, Irving. Now, don't you lie to me."

Irving lifts a finger, "I brought home something else delicious."

Irving disappears. I stand in the kitchen like an idiot. Which glasses do I get out? Whatever Irving brings out better require a glass; Maple candy, although delicious, is a poor substitute for bourbon.

Irving arrives with two wine bottles. "My friend, Andrew, made mead."

I get two wine glasses. Irving pours. The mead isn't sweet as I would like, but it gets the job done. As I polish off my second glass, Irving raises his eyebrows.

"Don't look at me like that!" I remark. "Drinking is the only pastime we enjoy together. Therefore, I'm going to enjoy it."

Irving's face becomes sincere. "There's a sense of sadness to that."

"Whose fault is that?" I mutter.

We pour glass after glass. I lose track of how much we drink. Irving drinks more that usual. That is saying a lot. Irving can down an entire bottle of wine on his own. The mead is gone. Irving opens the refrigerator.

"Do you, I mean, we have any beer?"

"Why are you asking me?" I giggle, "I've been in the woods for the last few weeks."

"I do not see it," Irving says as he shuts the refrigerator. "That is okay. I rather taste you."

In a flash, Irving lifts me with great strength despite his weak body. I squeal in shock. Irving carries me into my room. He throws me onto my bed with such force that I bounce. He strokes a finger from my lips to the waistband of my pants. It's a move too bold for Irving. He tugs at the band. "May I?"

It's not Irving! He's Joey!

I close my eyes so I could see Joey. He makes love to me with the gentle strength he possessed twenty years ago. My body spasms with pleasure. Joey goes for a long time. Eventually, I start heaving. I need to tap out. Joey releases with a grunt and Irving's dumpy lankiness rolls off of me.

I run to the bathroom and throw up. Two decades without an orgasm left my body unable to tolerate the many Joey wishes to give me. I brush my teeth and wash my face.

I enter my bedroom. Irving's body stares at the wall. "Are you still in there?"

"Barely," Irving answers.

I let out a disappointing, "Oh."

Irving sits up. "You know, I had a highly improbable dream. I stood there watching another man make love to you."

"Go to your room, Irving!"

Irving obliges. Walking pass me is the man I love to loathe. It isn't fair for either of us. Ours was never going to be a marriage as long my heart lays in Joey's ashes. I care, yet I don't.

I lay in bed. The familiar warmth washes over me. Joey holds me. I fall asleep.

22

I wake up to the sounds of Irving getting ready for work. The weight of Joey's spirit prevents me from getting up. He releases me as we hear Irving leaving the house. I get up, take a shower, the emerge from the bathroom to find a shirtless Joey in my kitchen.

"Do you think you would have remained so muscular have you lived?" I laugh.

Joey smirks, "Of course. You wouldn't expect me to slack off on the fitness."

I smile. The truth if Joey were standing in front of me alive, I'd take him with a 200 lb beer belly.

"I'd make you coffee," Joey says, "but I am severely impaired in this realm."

"I can make it."

I prep the coffee maker then get dressed. Joey is still here when I come out of my bedroom. He leans over the coffee pot.

"It stills smells good."

"I don't remember you drinking coffee when we were in school."

Joey shakes his head. "I drank sports drinks. Everyone else I know drank coffee. Some of my best times were spent at Caribou Coffee with friends. I wish we had some of those times."

Joey gazes out into a world I cannot see. I stare at him as I get the vanilla flavored almond milk I use in my coffee from the fridge. I spill it as I pour. Joey notices and shakes his head with a grin. I drink my coffee with a smile. It's all so natural, drinking coffee and staring at a shirtless Joey. This could have been my life.

"We could make this a weekly thing," I suggest.

Joey stops smiling. "Marion...."

"Winter is here. If we have a heavy snowfall here and there, Irving will stay home. I'll keep our liquor cabinet well stocked..."

Joey puts his hand out to silence me.

"Marion. Your awareness that I was making love to you this time made me want to stay in Irving's body too long. It's getting dangerous. One night, I may stay long enough to cause Irving's soul to separate from his body."

I set the coffee cup on the counter with shaky hands.

"Did you say 'this time'? Were there other times, Joey?"

"Joey was just as much my daughter as she was Irving's."

A daughter? I had a daughter. My knees buckle underneath me. Joey attempts to catch me, but I fall through him. I feel his warmth around me, but his muscular arms are illusions. I cry. My life could have been like this: a husband who comforts me when I am sad, a husband who I could make love to body and soul.

"I'm sorry, Marion," Joey whispers. "I am so sorry. I should have left you alone. I just couldn't. I died angry. I died angry at your father for setting me up and then angry that I couldn't be with you. I wanted to reclaim you. My return has caused you pain."

I wipe my eyes. "Can a body live without a soul?"

"No," Joey answers, "and Irving has a soul whether you want to believe it or not."

"Couldn't he use yours?"

"It's not how things work."

"If only..."

There is nothing to say. Joey's spirit returning can only show me what a life we could have. In reality, we can never be a fully engaged couple.

"What's the point of all this, Joey?"

"I love you."

Those words intended for comfort bring little of it.

"Are you considering leaving?" I ask, "What was the point of you coming back if you are only going to leave?"

Joey sighs. I feel his warm energy blow through my hair.

"My own selfish reasons," he answers, "You returned to me after your accident. Holding you awoke all these feelings I thought were dormant. You always were a hard one to let go."

"So are you."

Joey fades.

My anger doesn't fade. I go to work. Irving passes me on the staircase.

"Someone has a chip on her shoulder," he comments.

He has no idea. All I see is red. I am armed with an old key and the knowledge my father never moved his office during his entire tenure at Nicollet Community College. He is teaching comprehensive reading right now. I turn the key into the lock and enter the empty room.

I started my studies at Nicollet in my late twenties. Father poisoned my desire for higher learning; therefore, I knew I wasn't getting anything beyond my associate's degree. I picked a major conducive to a career, computer science.

Binary code is like riding a bike. I rarely utilize the language after graduation, but I can write it fluently when the need arises. Since my classes,

I engaged in extracurricular learning and can write code not taught in class.

Father's computer is an archaic desktop. He has yet to comply to the college's transition to tablet computers like the other instructors. For an intelligent man, Father puts his password on a sticky note under his keyboard. I login his computer and start typing 1s and 0s. Thankfully, I finish before I hear the sounds of footsteps coming down the hallway.

I exit hoping whoever is walking down the hall is not Father. Any other employee would think nothing of a daughter being her father's office. My father, whose footsteps I heard, does not. He eyes me suspiciously as I walk towards him and a young female student.

"I left the corrected registrations on your desk, Mr. Portwood," I lie.

"Uh, thank you," he says as I pass.

As soon as I turn the hall, I quicken my step. That cad! He speaks to me with no recognition, so the young student he is with doesn't know I'm his daughter. The girl is half my age! Of course, I could be making assumptions. I better get to my desk and figure it out.

From my computer, I type in more code. Father's video camera comes on. I put my earbuds in my ears and listen to Father quote maudlin sonnets while I work. The young female coos or give feeble responses such as "That's interesting." When the sounds become mistaken for pornography, and I am assured I won't be hearing the word "no," I lock my screen and go to lunch.

I return and save the video onto a flash drive. President Wester will come back to an anonymous envelope at her desk. My father will get the notice he will be meeting with the ethics board tomorrow.

23

"I hope you're satisfied!"

Irving walks into the house and drops his bag in the kitchen with a thud. I look up from my e-reader.

"I was," I answer, "until you made me lose my paragraph. Do you care to inform me what your little outburst was about?"

Irving stomps over to the kitchen table. The sounds of his boots against floor are ominous. When I look up at Irving's face, I need to bite my lip not to laugh. Irving looks ridiculous with his short stature standing erected over my chair. He reminds me of a little boy trying to imitate his angry parent.

"Dr. Wester and the ethics board revoked your father's tenure and terminated his employment!"

"Oh my," I say nonchalantly.

"You can't even fake surprise at the news!"

"Consequences have actions, Irving."

Irving raises his hands in the air. "Are you drunk? It's actions have consequences."

"I am not drunk," I reply, "and I am stand by what I said."

For years, my father sought consequences for those he thought the worse. He had Joey hunted for running away with his underage girlfriend. He called the police on my mother's pot smoking. Father received no consequences for his immoral actions. It was time for me to take action.

Irving doesn't bother to take off his coat. He walks to the fridge and pulls out an open bottle of Chardonnay. I didn't know we had that. Irving pours himself a glass without offering me one.

"You're not a naïve girl, Marion...."

"I'm not a girl," I interject, " I got my tits awhile ago."

Pretending to read, I watch Irving's face contort in angry expressions. A small smile escapes my lips.

"Point is, Marion, you knew of your father's activities for some time. What I don't understand is why it bothers you now. And for you to hand him over as fodder to Dr. Wester as you did...Marion, I just don't get it."

"Exactly what extreme action you implying, Irving?"

Irving slams his glass on the counter with a hard thud. I am surprised it didn't shatter.

"Quit playing dumb, Marion! Despite your jaunt in the woods, you are the most tech savvy girl I know. Yes, I meant to say girl! I haven't been blind to your passive aggressive rants towards your father. I saw every eye roll and heard every condensing one-word answer you give him. Rather disrespectful considering what you put him through."

Now I roll my eyes at Irving. "Don't talk of subjects that you have little information about. You'll only sound like an idiot."

Irving leans forward on the counter with a dramatic sigh. Like any other man, he believes he can engage in theatrics without being subjected to ridicule. His next stunt is taking a long sip of wine that depletes the glass's contents.

"Say what you want about your father, Marion. He is still a brilliant man. Your stunt cost many young minds a great deal."

"Brilliance is open to interpretation. Besides, many think Roman Polanski as brilliant, yet that doesn't change the fact he is a sexual deviant."

Irving turns his head towards me. "All those girls were of age, Marion."

I put my e-reader down. "Age doesn't matter, Irving. All employees have to abide by the Nicollet College code of ethics. I think the real reason you are mad is that you have gone against the code as well. You are shaming me to deflect the blame you share with my father. Rest assured, Irving, I don't care about you enough which way or the other to rat you out."

I pick up my e-reader feeling Irving's eyes shooting proverbial lasers in my direction. I feel heat upon my face where he gazes. He slaps the counter.

"Tell me this, Marion. If you have little regard for me, why are we married?"

"Because you and Father are in love each other. Our marriage allows the two of you to form a union as heterosexual men."

"That is ridiculous!"

"Truly? Is it really?"

Irving's face vigorously contorts as he tries to come up with a pithy retort. It smooths when he realizes he can't think of one. I stand up from my chair.

"Irving, why are we doing this? Why are we in this marriage?"

"Marion, not now," Irving replies. "I know we are bound to have this conversation but not now."

"You know?" I ask, "how long have you known."

"Since the day we got married."

I let out a bewildered laugh. "Seriously! Irving, we've been married for better part of a decade!"

"I am fond of you, Marion."

"Fondness isn't love."

"True," Irving replies, "but it still can lead to a content companionship."

Irving wipes his face with his hands. Is he crying? I could never tell with him. Another looming red flag, I know.

"The accident awoke me, Irving. Things that I tolerated before I no longer can. I can't be complacent anymore I can't live with mere fondness. If I can't have love, I rather be alone and live according to my rules."

Irving stares at me. He doesn't reach for my hand. He doesn't protest that I am wrong and he actually does love me. He doesn't move to embrace me. He stands there.

"If you are worried that the end of our marriage will result in terminating your relationship with my father, I assure you it won't. In fact, our divorce will only strengthen your bond. I am enemy number one after all."

I go to my room and pack my larger duffle bag. Irving follows me, watches me, but doesn't say anything. When I complete my packing, I say, "You can keep the house. There is nothing I care for here."

I go down stairs. When I reach the door, I hear "Marion, stop."

I turn around.

"There are many reasons to love you," Irving says.

"But you didn't", I say opening the door.

"It wasn't for lack of wanting."

 "Goodbye, Irving."

I walk out and shut the door.

****

I stand outside Mother's trailer. After five knocks she answers.

"Marion? Is everything all right?"

"Yes. I got Father fired from Nicollet College."

Mother's eyes arch. "Let me guess; you need a place to hideout."

"Yes, please."

Mother opens the door with a swooping gesture.

"Stay as long as you need to," she says. "The guest room is where it's always been."

I proceed to the guest room I stayed many times in my childhood. The woven blankets and the smell of moth balls bring back memories. Tonight I can stay and hide from the future I have to face.

24

Irving says Father put the house on the market the day after I left. He spends his final two weeks at Nicollet stalking me during my lunch. He takes an interest in me now that our marriage is over.

"You're different," he says every time we have lunch.

Of course I'm different. I am freer. Now that I am no longer Irving's wife, I'm able to overlook his flaws and find him a pleasant lunch companion. I just smile in response.

Irving quit his job. He will move with Father to Vermont once the house gets sold. They will try to get teaching jobs there. If they are unsuccessful, my aunt has an orchard where they could work. Father won't talk to me. Frankly, I don't care.

"You really ought to make peace with him," Irving says. "He is your father. I understand you disagree with how he demonstrated his love, but he did care about you."

"I'm sure that he believes that."

"He does," Irving replies, "I hope you will communicate with him sometime soon. I also hope you keep in contact with me. I want to stay friends."

"We can," I say.

In reality, I have no intention of fostering a real friendship with Irving. He's nice, but our personalities aren't compatible. If he really does find me fascinating now, why didn't he stand up against Father on my behalf? True,

I needed to fight my battles. Still, life could have been easier if I had a supportive life partner.

"Well, I have to go," I say, "There are last minute changes to the spring semester schedule I have the attend to."

"I'm sorry about that," Irving says with a sheepish smile.

"Good luck," I say.

I walk into my cubicle rolling my eyes at Irving's apology. He's not the one fixing hundreds of students schedules. I'll be working through Christmas undoing his mess and Father's mess as well.

Mother works nights. There is an hour at the most when we are in the trailer at the same time. I don't mind. As adults, our exchanges are awkward. Living with a criminal record harden Mother. She doesn't approach me with tenderness as she did in my youth. She still makes sure I eat. Every night she brings two bags of leftovers from the Wana Yi Lake buffet.

One night she comes home with a bag of spare ribs with a box of cheesecake. I sit at the table as she pulls the take out cartons out.

"I don't celebrate Christmas much," she says.

"I don't prefer making Christmas a big deal," I reply.

"I have to work both tomorrow and Christmas Day," Mother advises, "but if you come around to the buffet, I can get Tom to comp your dinner. I can join you on my break."

"Whatever you like," I say, "We can talk more as the day draws near."

Mother sits down, "Marion, tomorrow is Christmas Eve."

I have enough things to keep track of that I forget what day it is. Irving may want to remain friends after the divorce, but Father is not above manipulating him to get back at me. Father already convinced Irving to sell family heirlooms so I wouldn't get my hands on them. I don't care about Grandma Irving's wedding china. I just need half its monetary value.

"I understand if you forgot," Mother says, "you have enough to worry about."

"Well, thankfully the gift I want from you has no cost."

"Oh really now?"

"You changed your name back to Larson after your divorce, right."

Mother sits down, "Not right away. I was in the process of getting my felony conviction at the time of the divorce."

"That's right," I say sheepishly.

Mother nods and walks proceeds to eat.

"It's just I'm not too terribly attached to Palavar," I continue, "but I don't want to go back to being a Portwood. Also, I was born equally a Larson as I was a Portwood."

"True," Mother replies, "you were."

"So, if possible, I would like your blessing to change my name to Larson when I finalize the divorce."

A small smile escapes Mother's lips. Still, she maintains her namesake's stoic nature.

"You don't need my blessing for that," Mother says. "You said it yourself; the name is equally yours. Take it if you like."

"Are you sure?"

"Marion, I am glad you know I am not into Christmas with its materialistic commercialism. Don't play this off as I am giving you your half of you birth right to assuage your obligation to celebrate the holiday. Take it."

"Well I..."

"While we are on the topic," Mother cut in, "don't be obligated to get me anything for Christmas. I don't do gifts."

"Very well," I say.

Mother scoffs at my Englishness. We eat the rest of the meal in silence.

The trailer park is alive on Christmas Day. The neighborhood is lit with Christmas lights and bonfires. Instead of singing Christmas carols, neighbors drum and sing the songs of our people. Mother leaves for work. I grab my coat and join the festivities.

I walk around. I receive looks and awkward smiles as I walk around the park. This isn't a whitie on the Rez type of thing. I am related to most of the people out here. It's an awkward family reunion where neither party knows who should approach who first. A car pulling next to Mother's trailer is a saving grace, especially since Marty exits the car!

I try not to run. I don't want to appear eager. I busied myself with work and the divorce so I wouldn't think of Marty. I missed him all these weeks. I just didn't want to admit it.

"Wow," he says when he sees me. "Sounds like quite the party out there."

"I suppose," I answer with a small smile.

Yes, the party is jovial. I should make an effort to get reacquainted with my family; but, I'm selfish. I just want to be with Marty, alone.

"Do you want to come in? I could make tea or coffee?"

"Anything's fine."

I open the door and motion for Marty to walk in. He sniffs the air. Mother's morning joint still lingers in the kitchen.

"It's a spiritual…"

Marty cuts in, "Who am I to judge?"

Marty sits down at the kitchen table.

"Would you like tea or coffee?"

"Coffee," Marty answers, "I'm not much of a tea drinker; although, I shouldn't be drinking it this late. I'll be up all night."

I search the shelves. "I think we have decaf somewhere."

I find an old canister of decaffeinated Folgers from the time of Grandmother Larson. It can't be fresh. Mother doesn't buy the fancy flavor creamers to mask the taste. I stick with brewing the caffeinated coffee.

As much as I like looking at Marty's soft face, I find it easier to form cohesive sentences with my back turned to him. "I thought you were in California."

"I was," Marty says. "I convinced Mom that I had a good project in the Midwest. She came to visit and decided it's not the place for her. I don't know what to do. I know her days are numbered."

I pour coffee in green mugs. They are the only cups seeming festive for the day.

"Are you going back?"

Marty thanks me for the coffee then continues. "I may have to. The thing is the jobs are out here. I get paid the best in the Midwest, and it's how I afford her care. Now, there is a comparable job in Arizona which isn't too far from California. I don't know."

"A tough situation," I comment.

"She's all I have, my mom," Marty says, "Enough about me. How are you?"

"Similar to you," I say sitting down, "I am faced with a bunch of unknowns."

"You live here now?" Marty asks.

"Yes," I say, "the winter storm made it impossible to get in or out of the treehouse. I guess it will have to be a three seasons dwelling."

"You made peace with your mom. She lets you live in her home."

161

"Well, yes," I answer, "how did you know where to find me?"

"I saw her at the casino yesterday. She told me where to find you."

"Really now? She said yesterday she didn't do Christmas presents."

Now comes the dreaded awkward pause. There is a lot to talk about. Will telling him I missed him scare him off? Do I mention Irving? Is it wise to bring up his wife? Do we really need to process our last night together? Are we just going to be incredibly awkward to the point we may never see each other after tonight?

Marty breaks the silence. "I'm sorry I left things they way I did after Thanksgiving."

"Well," I answer, "it must be awkward when the woman you're with claims to see your dead cousin."

"Aien't going to deny that," Marty replies. "I don't know. I guess hearing you say you saw him made me realize I got too wrapped up with the treehouse. I wasn't sure I liked you because Joey liked you or I missed my wife. I needed space because I am just confused."

"Why did you build the treehouse?"

Marty stares into his cup. "My wife died in a car accident three years ago. A drunk driver went straight speeding down the wrong exit ramp. He killed our baby too."

"Are you saying she was pregnant?"

"Yeah."

The similarities between our situations are chilling. Do I mention that? No, now is not the time. There may never be a time to bring up Irving and my baby. I nod for Marty to continue.

"I dated my wife when Joey came to Anaheim. She was with us when the bounty hunter found him and…"

Marty wipes away tears.

"She was there when Joey died," I say with a pang of jealousy.

Marty sadly laughs. "She tried to stop the bounty hunter. She got on his back and started hitting him. I went to her when the bounty hunter pushed her off. Maybe if I went to help Joey, he might be…"

"Maybe you'd be dead too," I comment.

"After Joey died, she never left my side. I was a bear to be around. I'd drink. Sometimes, she got the brunt of my anger. No matter how much I shout at her, she stayed. I can't believe she wanted to marry me after all that. She was a great gal. Too bad you left right away at the memorial service. You could have met her."

"The memorial service?" I question, "were you the one who made sure I received some of Joey's ashes?"

Marty nods. We sit in silence. Marty wipes his eyes. A firecracker from outside thunders too close to the trailer.

Marty attempts to laugh, Punk kids, uh?"

"Every neighborhood got some."

Marty stares at his cup.

"Shane. Her name was Shane."

"That's a lovely name," I reply.

"Shane believed in psychics. I didn't, I mean not she was alive. My first month out here, someone suggested I go to Stillwater for a day trip. There was this antique shop that rented a corner to a psychic. I figured what the hell? Shane believed in them. Maybe she'll talk to me through the psychic.

"The psychic starts asking me if I know a Joey. She told me he was coming in, asking for me to build a house in the woods for Marion. I threw her some money and ran out. I haven't thought of Joey much since Shane's death. I hate to say it; I hardly remembered your name. The fact the woman knew both names freaked me out.

"I have to be honest, Minnesota is not the greatest place to make new friends. I spend a lot of my time alone in my room. I started making designs for your house. I looked up zoning laws. I had these dreams where Joey walks me to the hill. It's a place the city will never let me build. Still, night after night, I dreamt of Joey. Finally, I obtained some construction barricades and started working. It's weird how everyone just minds their own business here. I never got questioned once."

"Even when you brought machinery into the woods?"

"I didn't," Marty answers. "That is why you didn't have a bathroom. Joey's goal was for a house to blend into the woods."

"Like our fort."

Marty nods.

"Building a house for someone you don't know while grieving shows a lot of character."

Marty shrugs. "It wasn't entirely selfless. Working on the house diverted my mind from the pain. Joey was the good-looking sports star, but I felt sorry for him. I had both my parents and Shane. He didn't have anyone real in his life but you. Building the tree house was my way to make it up to him."

Now I know it. I can love Marty.

"Bloomington Lincoln had lots of cute jocks," I say, "I never gave them the time of day. Joey was different. He was loving and sincere. You're just like him in the ways that matter."

Marty gives me a small smile. "Thanks."

I need to say something more. Drumming my fingers on the table doesn't drum up the courage. Marty gets up.

"I should," Marty says, "I should just leave and let you have your Christmas."

I shoot up from my chair. "I wish you won't."

Marty stops. He looks at me, expecting me to announce why I stopped him. It's now or never. I pray I don't sound like a babbling idiot.

"I loved Joey. You have everything I love about him. I know you're not Joey. Joey was my past and if there is a chance…"

Marty smiles awkwardly. I've said too much.

"You were saying?"

I shake my head. "Nevermind."

Marty steps forward. "Go on. I like what you're saying."

"I don't know what could become of us, but I want to find out."

Marty steps towards me. He kisses me.

"I'll be in Minnesota until April," he says. "I'll call you tomorrow. We can start seeing where this all goes then."

We kiss, and Marty leaves. I wave from the window as he drives away. Once he is gone, I run around the trailer, jumping on furniture, and screaming with excitement. My life will finally be a life worth living. No matter what happens between Marty and me, I will get to discover what will make me happy.

25

"This may be what you need," I say.

Dr. Kroll follows me into the treehouse. It's now mid-April. The melting snow makes the mud to soft. In my delicate condition, that's a bad thing. Dr. Kroll's slender frame is barely capable of breaking my fall. Luckily, we made it up the muddy hill without incident.

Dr. Kroll walks around the house. He touches the frame of the daybed.

"You slept here?" he asks, "you actually lived here."

"I couldn't shower here," I answer, "but I could do everything else required for civilized living. Although, I moved to my mother's before the weather got frigid. I don't know how I would be able to use the outhouse in below zero temperatures."

"I see," Dr. Kroll replies. "Did staying in the woods help you as you say it did?"

"Why would I say it did if it didn't?"

"True."

Dr. Kroll continues to walk around. He hopes the house will heals his wife as it healed me.

After New Year's, Dr. Kroll canceled an appointment. He disappeared for two months. I didn't give his absence much thought. It's not like I really needed him. Not having to leave his office in a state of confusion every week was a welcomed change. Marty filled up my spare time and always left me satisfied.

Last month, Dr. Kroll called. I was in a crisis of change at that time, but he didn't want to talk about me. Little did I know, we'd be switching roles.

"My wife attempted suicide," he said the moment I sat down in his office.

"Oh my! I am sorry to hear that."

Dr. Kroll sat bent over looking at the floor. His hair flopped over his eyes. Patches of stubble scattered across his face. A sweatshirt replaced his usual sweater. He was in crisis. Compared to him, I just put myself in a complicated situation.

"I knew she was unhappy," he began. "I thought the worst scenario would be her leaving me. She said the same things you said. She didn't feel like she was enough. I brushed her comments off as banal insecurities. I worked a lot and mistook her remarks as a ploy for attention."

He put his head in his hand. I sat with my hands gripping the arms of the chair. Dr. Kroll's actions were entirely inappropriate. Yet, I realized the man had to be in enormous pain to turn to me.

"Come now," I say, "Many a man made the same assumption you did."

"That is why many marriages end in divorce," Dr. Kroll remarked, "and that is a better scenario."

I let Dr. Kroll cry. Thankfully, none of the other practitioners heard him down the hall. Dr. Kroll crossed serious boundaries. Ethics boards often forget their purpose was to protect humans. Any other medical professional would punish Kroll for being one. That never seemed right to me.

Dr. Kroll calmed down. He looked at me. "You revived your will to live after decades of being suicidal. How did you do that?"

"I wouldn't say I was suicidal the entire time," I replied, "I eventually became numb to the world around me. That is no way to live. Hopefully, it doesn't have to be that way for your wife."

"But how?"

Dr. Kroll was the man who was supposed to have all the answers. I kept the bemused chuckling in my head. From the last two decades, I knew that canned therapeutic practices don't work. Dr. Kroll put his professional faith in them. Now his wife is in distress, and he is clueless to help her. I feel bad that I find this amusing.   *present tense*

"I found evidence that Joey truly loved me," I said, "Maybe your wife needs to know you love her."

"If it were that simple, the suicide rate would be minimal," Dr. Kroll remarked. "Just about everyone committing suicide has people who love them."

"Still, you should be talking to your wife instead of me," I said getting up. "How can you expect to help her if you don't know what she is feeling? Good day, Dr. Kroll."

As I turned towards the door, Dr. Kroll asked, "Are you pregnant?"

Despite Marty's and my agreement to proceed with the relationship slowly, we didn't impede our physical relationship. A month later, we discovered the life changing results to our folly, dumbfounded like two teenagers. Needless to say, there was a lot to process in regards to starting a family with Marty. I couldn't talk about that with a man who barely could handle his own feelings with his wife. I left.

A few weeks later, Dr. Kroll called me again. He mentioned he noticed the biggest change in my demeanor when I left Irving.

"Let me show you a place that could help you and your wife."

Now Dr. Kroll scrutinizes every nook and cranny of the treehouse. "It's small."

"A person doesn't need much," I say. "With the entire length of the creek as your yard, you don't need material things for entertainment."

Dr. Kroll sighs. I still don't have the full story on what drove his wife to attempt suicide. Just because escaping to the treehouse healed me, she may not have the same resolution. I sense what Dr. Kroll is not saying: he is casing the place to assess if it is viable for two people.

"I remember reading your first suicide attempt happened in the nearby creek."

"True," I say, "but my health grew worse when Father kept me away."

Dr. Kroll grunts.

"Alcoholism is prevalent among my mother's people," I say. "The elders say it is because we are forced to live a life removed from the earth. It only creates madness. Hence a person does what they can to become numb."

"A Hollywood star blogged about walking barefoot outside. She called it 'earthing.' Sounds like hogwash that could have some merit."

"I was shocked at what I could achieve in a minimalist house," I reply. "Overcoming hurdles of modern life, and pushing away the unnecessary burdens gave me a sense of purpose. Once I had that, things started falling into place."

Dr. Kroll looks into the closet.

"Of course, you have first to be prepared to acknowledge your wife's feelings," I went on. "If you don't do that, anything else is meaningless. I know if people validated my love for Joey, I'd never attempt suicide."

"It's not that simple for everyone," Dr. Kroll says.

"But you will never achieve health if you refuse to begin with the basics."

Dr. Kroll shuts the closet door.

"I won't be coming around here anymore," I say. "I leave Minnesota in a week. I know spirits will guide a needy soul here. But, I just want to know someone is making good use of the place. You sounded like you were at a loss with your wife. This treehouse may be an option."

"There is a lot to think about," Dr. Kroll says.

I leave him with his thoughts. I will not know the outcome of his marriage. I have to think of my child.

Marty's mother demanded we move to California when he told her we were expecting. Marty had to complete the contract with the Mall of America. Towards the last couple of months, the company in Arizona made an attractive offer. Marty convinced his mother to compromise and move to Arizona. We will rent a house for the four of us. Marty prefers I stay home with the baby. I am not one to tie my identity to my job. Joey, the baby I lost, made me realize how much I wanted to be a mother.

Mother helps me pack. She tries to hide her disappointment that I am moving. She understands the situation. I insist Marty and I will come back after his mom dies. She shakes her head at my attempts to assure her.

"The baby is going to revive Marty's mother. She'll live an extra year or two than expected."

more

"I have hoped you'd be close to teach the baby the traditions of your people," I say.

Mother closes my suitcase. "I am going to be in the child's life, aren't I?"

"Yes. Of course."

"Then the child will learn the traditions of our people," she says. "Just promise me one thing."

"Sure."

"I get a photo taken every year with my grandchild."

"I'll try to come back."

"Good," Mother replies. "I need something to send to your aunt in Vermont."

We laugh.

Mother doesn't give a sappy goodbye. She helps me in the U-haul Marty rented. She waves us off. Maybe she'll appreciate having a home to herself away from the awkwardness of repairing our relationship. Will she miss me?

Marty and I drive for two days. The baby has grown enough to cause bladder discomfort. We have to stop every hour.

I insisted we take the road coming into Phoenix from the north. There is a place I longed to go.

I am driving when the road signs announce my desire location. Marty sleeps in the passenger seat. I turn off the GPS so that it doesn't shout at me for going off the route. Following the road signs, I reach the Grand Canyon and all of its splendor.

Marty wakes up as I park the car. "Is this the Canyon?"

"Yes," I answer, "ever been here?"

"Shane and I honeymooned here."

"Joey and I planned to celebrate my eighteenth birthday here," I say. "Twenty years later, I made it."

I get out of the car and go to the lookout point.

"Should you be going out there?" Marty asks.

"I'll be fine."

It's an hour before sunset, the magic hour. The sky is a technicolor blue. The sun causes the Canyon to glow in various shades of pink and orange. This place could easily be heaven.

I see a man with black hair standing by the rail overlooking the drop. He turns around. It's Joey!

Joey nods to Marty then to me. He starts walking up into the sky. This time is the last I will see Joey during my time on earth. He loves me enough to let me go.

I'll die in my old age. I'll return to an expanded heaven with the Grand Canyon overlooking the beauty of Miles Creek below. I'll be survived by my daughter, Dakota, and her five children. Marty will be waiting for me along with Joey and Shane. It will be a great day, but not as great as today.

I turn to Marty. He is not Joey. He will be the one I'll spend the majority of my life with, our love growing over time. He is more than enough for me. I reach my hand to him. He walks over to me. He takes my hand. I reach into my purse with the other. I pull out the white box with the cross.

"Joey's ashes?" Marty asks.

"It was hard to let him go," I say, "should we release him together?"

Marty places his hand underneath mine. Together we toss Joey's cremains in the air. A strong gust of wind scatters them around the Canyon.

Marty and I kiss. We move on.

ABOUT THE AUTHOR

S. Collin Ellsworth is the author of the novels "Answered" and "Finding the Route 40 Phantom". She is the host of the podcast, "10,000 Lakes 10,000,000 Books: Conversations with Minnesota Authors". Ms. Ellsworth graduated from Minnesota State University Moorhead. She is a member of Toastmasters International, Chanhassen Authors Collective, The Art Consortium of Carver County and is a Girl Scout Troop Leader. Ms. Ellsworth lives with her family in Bloomington, MN.

Made in the USA
Lexington, KY
22 July 2017